Hot color rushed into her cheeks but the laser burn of her eyes did not waver from his. "I thought you were committed to an easy come, easy go mindset."

"I don't have a one-night stand in mind this time around."

"I think you'd better lay out what you do have in mind, Nick, because I am feeling distinctly lost on the road you've just taken."

Just one night with Tess had demonstrated how addictive she could be—experiencing the whole package of her—and Nick instinctively shied from ceding that control to any woman. However, if he could keep things reasonable...and Tess was a very reasonable woman...

The incredulous note in her voice was warning enough that she'd find his proposal completely off the wall, but it had to be put on the table and the sooner it was done, the better, giving him a platform to move forward with her.

"Not an affair, Tess. I was thinking more along the lines of us getting married and having a child together."

Three popular Harlequin Presents® authors
bring you an exciting new miniseries:

The Ramirez Brides

*Three half brothers, scattered to opposite sides
of the globe: each must find a bride
in order to find each other....*

Book 1: *The Ramirez Bride* by Emma Darcy

Australian billionaire Nick Ramirez must find a
wife and produce an heir within a year. Though
many women have shared his bed, there's only
one he'd choose to be his Ramirez Bride....

Look out for the next two titles in this trilogy—
coming soon!

Book 2: *The Brazilian's Blackmailed Bride*
by Michelle Reid
October 2005 #2493

Book 3: *The Disobedient Virgin*
by Sandra Marton
November 2005 #2499

Available only from Harlequin Presents®!

Emma Darcy

THE RAMIREZ BRIDE

The Ramirez Brides

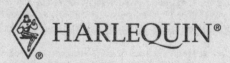

HARLEQUIN®

TORONTO • NEW YORK • LONDON
AMSTERDAM • PARIS • SYDNEY • HAMBURG
STOCKHOLM • ATHENS • TOKYO • MILAN • MADRID
PRAGUE • WARSAW • BUDAPEST • AUCKLAND

ISBN 0-373-12487-2

THE RAMIREZ BRIDE

First North American Publication 2005.

www.eHarlequin.com

Printed in U.S.A.

CHAPTER ONE

A PACKET from Brazil…delivered by a courier fulfilling instructions to have Nick Ramirez himself sign for it so that delivery to him personally was assured, no chance of it being mislaid and not reaching him…this packet from Brazil.

Nick watched the courier leave his office, his gaze fixed on the man's back, on the door closing behind him. He didn't want to look at the packet now lying on his desk, didn't want to open it. The hand that had directed it to him had to be the hand of his father, his biological father, who had not earned the right to touch his life in any way whatsoever, let alone force an entry to it. That door had been closed sixteen years ago.

No. Earlier than that.

Much earlier.

Nick was thirty-four now and he'd only been seven when the sense of rejection had hit him full force from all sides. The memory of himself as a young schoolboy not understanding anything, stirred Nick out of his chair, an angry shot of adrenaline energising a move away from the packet from Brazil. At seven he'd been a complete innocent, caught in a web of adult deceptions, trying to find out where he fitted, and the brutal truth had been…he didn't fit.

Anywhere.

So he'd learnt to make his own place.

And this office was part of *his place*, the driving centre of the advertising company that occupied two floors of this prestigious building at Circular Quay with its commanding view of Sydney Harbour. It was Nick's company. His alone. He'd built it up, pursuing his concept of what the market would respond to and he'd been proved right. Spectacularly right.

As he stood at the window, looking out at the opera house and the huge coathanger span of the bridge behind it, Nick sardonically reflected that everyone knew sex sold. Sex and glamour. But he knew it very personally, so much so he had the knack of packaging it better than anyone else, constructing impact shots that were highly memorable, fixing the target product in people's minds. His style of advertising had made him a very wealthy man, well able to afford this million-dollar view, both in his work-place and the penthouse apartment he owned at Woolloomooloo.

Here he was, standing on top of his world, totally self-sufficient, a successful man in his own right. He didn't need anything from any of his *fathers*—the rich, powerful men his mother had attracted, drawing from them whatever her covetous heart desired.

Over the years of his boyhood and adolescence they'd shelled out a lot to him, as well, wanting to please her. He'd used the money to fund his aims and ambition. Why not? He'd earned it by not being a pest in their lives.

But he didn't *take* anything from any one any more.

Didn't need to.

Didn't want to.

And it was far too late for Enrique Ramirez to offer him anything. The Brazilian had had two chances to make a difference in Nick's life. He'd walked away from the first. As for the second, when Nick had turned up in Rio de Janeiro—an eighteen-year-old youth seeking to acquaint himself with a father he'd never known—he'd been met with furious resentment at the sheer impudence of presenting himself as Enrique's son in the man's own home.

'What do you want from me? What do you imagine you can get out of me?'

The jeering contempt from the highly placed Brazilian had stung Nick into replying, 'Nothing. I just wanted to meet you in person. But I *will* take your name. I can see now it belongs to me.'

There was no denying the genetic pattern that had clearly been passed on to him—the same thick black hair and distinctive hairline, dark olive skin, deeply set green eyes with double-thick lashes, a long aristocratic nose, high angular cheekbones, hard squarish jawline broken by a central cleft that probably should have weakened the forceful impression of aggressive masculinity but perversely enough lent a rakish power to it, a mouth that was carved for sensuality, and the tall muscular physique combining both strength and athleticism.

Oh yes, he was his father's son all right. And when he'd returned home to Australia he had claimed the name, Ramirez, by deed-poll. At least, that wasn't a lie. But whatever the packet from Brazil contained…Nick was already rebelling against any effect Enrique might think he could have on him.

His desk telephone rang.

A few strides back from the window and he snatched up the receiver.

'Mrs Condor is on the line, wanting to speak to you,' his PA informed.

His mother. Which made two unwelcome parental intrusions this morning. A sense of black irony tipped

Nick into saying, 'Put her through.' A click, then his dry invitation to converse, 'Mother?'

'Darling! Something extraordinary has happened. We must speak.'

'We are speaking.'

'I mean get together. Can you fit me in this morning? I'm on my way into the city now. It is important, Nick. I've received a packet from Brazil.'

Nick's jaw tightened at this news. 'So did I,' he bit out.

'Oh!' The sound of surprise and disappointment. 'Well, I was going to break it to you gently since he was your father, but I guess I don't need to now.' A dramatic sigh. 'Such a waste! Enrique could only have been in his sixties. Far too young for a man like him to die. He was so virile, so indomitable…'

A weird pain shafted Nick's heart.

His mind recoiled from the knowledge that Enrique Ramirez was dead.

Gone.

Never to be known as a son should know his father.

No more chances.

He stared at the packet on his desk—the last contact!

'He has gifted me the most magnificent emerald necklace…'

Pleasure in her voice as she proceeded to gloatingly describe every detail of it. His mother adored beautiful things. And she had certainly taught Nick the worth of sexy glamour. Every man who'd shared her bed— husband or lover—had paid for the privilege very handsomely indeed.

She was on her fifth marriage now, and if some more challenging mega-rich guy came along, Nick had little doubt her beautiful and highly acquisitive golden eyes would rove again. Though she hadn't snagged Enrique Ramirez as a husband.

In actual fact, she probably hadn't wanted to marry a Brazilian and settle in a very foreign country, anyway. It had undoubtedly been enough that the international polo-player had happened to be a judge in the Miss Universe contest, held in Rio de Janeiro the year Nadia Kilman had won that title.

Of course, she hadn't meant to get pregnant by him. That had been an unfortunate accident, especially when she was planning to marry Brian Steele, the son and heir of Australian mining magnate, Andrew Steele. But, easy enough for a woman of her persuasive charms to let the husband of her choice think he was the father of the child in her womb. It had certainly nailed a wedding to the targeted home-grown billionaire bridegroom.

Marriage had meant she had to give up her year as Miss Universe, but having won the title, his mother had never relinquished it and always—still—lived up to it.

The whole history of their mother-son relationship marched through Nick's mind as she raved on about the Ramirez emerald mines in Bolivia as though he had some legitimate claim on them. His mother specialised in making convenient claims.

Nick wondered if he would have remained Brian Steele's son if she had not been caught out in the lie. Even after the divorce and with both his parents remarried, Nick had still believed Brian Steele was his natural father, finally fronting up to him to demand why he didn't visit him at school, attending sporting events as other divorced fathers did.

'Ask your mother,' had been his harshly dismissive reply.

'It's not my fault you don't love my mother any more,' Nick had argued with a fierce sense of injustice. 'I'm not only her son. I'm *yours*, too.'

'No, you're not.'

Shocked, hurt, angry, Nick had fought against such an unfair and outright rejection. 'You can't divorce children. You're my father. Just because you've started another family doesn't mean...'

'I'm not your father.' The denial had been thundered back at Nick in red-faced rage. 'I was never your father. For God's sake, boy! Look at yourself in a mirror. There's not a trace of me in you.'

This further punch of shock had been countered by a rush of disbelief. It was true he didn't have red hair, fair skin or blue eyes, but he'd simply assumed he'd inherited his mother's darker colouring, and that was what his father hated in him—the constant reminder of her.

'You just don't want me, do you?' he'd flung out, tasting the bitterness of being the victim of a broken marriage, yet still intent on making his father face up to being his father.

'No, I don't. Why would I want another man's bastard as my son? Your real father's name is Enrique Ramirez and when he's not playing international polo, he lives in Brazil. I doubt *he* will ever visit your school to watch you play sport but you can try asking your mother to get in touch with him on your behalf.'

Having absorbed this new parentage and with seven-year-old determination, Nick had tried.

'Darling, I'm sorry you're upset about Brian not being your father.' His mother's brilliantly sympathetic smile had glossed over the dark wound he'd been nursing, as did her next words. 'But you have a perfectly good stepfather in Harry who's much more fun to have around...'

'I want to know about my real father,' he had bored in stubbornly.

'Well, he's married, dear. No chance at all of a divorce, I'm afraid. All wrapped up in the religion and politics of his country.' Her graceful hands had fluttered appealingly. 'So we can never form a family even if we wanted to.'

'Does he know about me?'

'Yes, he does.' A rueful sigh. 'One of those unlucky coincidences in life. He came out to Australia to play polo and your grandfather—well, he's not really your grandfather as you obviously realise now—invited him to play on his country property near Singleton, having built himself a private polo ground and fancying himself quite an accomplished player. It was a huge festive weekend. Impossible to get out of going. And I did think Enrique would be discreet and pretend not to know me.' Another sigh. 'It was seeing you that caught him off-guard.'

'He recognised me as his son?'

'Well, there was the matter of timing. Your age, as well as how you look, dear. The two things together... I had to admit it to him...and he used the secret to...uh...'

Blackmail her into bed with him.

And that was all Nick had meant to his biological father—a handy by-blow who'd given him the leverage to have his way with the ex-Miss Universe again. Though Nick suspected the arrogantly handsome and charismatic Brazilian had not needed much leverage.

Never mind the risk of scandal they'd both run. Never mind the fall-out for Nick when both their old and current affairs had been discovered.

'Your mother was as hot for me as I was for her,' Enrique had blithely excused when Nick had eventually laid out to him the consequences of his actions. Not a twinge of guilt to be seen. He'd thrown out elegantly dismissive hands. 'She could have said no. I have never made love to an unwilling woman. It was her choice. Her life.'

'And *my* life was irrelevant to you,' Nick had shot at him accusingly.

Enrique had snapped his fingers at what he considered a stupid complaint. 'I gave you life. Get on with finding pleasure in it. This dragging through the past will bring you no joy whatsoever.'

Good advice.

Nick had taken it.

Which was why he still didn't want to touch the packet from Brazil.

'What did he gift to you, darling?' his mother finally queried, her honeyed voice lilting with avid curiosity. The emerald necklace had certainly whetted her appetite for more treasure from Brazil.

'I'd say most of my physical features,' Nick mocked.

'True, dear, but that's not what I meant and you know it. Don't be tiresome. He wrote me that the necklace was a token of gratitude for having borne him such an impressive son. Obviously, if Enrique was pleased with you, he'd leave you much more than a necklace.'

'I haven't opened the packet yet.'

'Well, do get on with it, Nick. I expect to hear all

when I get to your office. This is so exciting I can hardly wait. Your father was fabulously wealthy, you know.'

Yes, he knew, having seen the incredible riches displayed in Enrique's home—a veritable treasure trove everywhere one looked—old, old wealth, the kind that belonged to aristocracy and was kept in the family, passed on from father to son.

But Nick didn't want it. His whole body burned to reject everything attached to the life that had meant so much more to his father than getting to know or playing any part in the life of his bastard son.

'I should be there in fifteen minutes,' his mother archly warned, clearly anticipating a happy sharing time together. 'Isn't it wonderful to be remembered like this after all these years?'

As always, she was totally self-centred in her view of the world and every situation in it. Nick was niggled into drawling, 'No, it isn't *wonderful*, Mother. I actually find it grossly insulting for my father to wait until he's dead before granting me some acknowledgement.'

'Oh, don't be stuffy, Nick. What's gone is gone. You should always make the most of what you've got.'

The rock-like principle on which Nadia Kilman/Steele/Manning/Lloyd/Hardwick/Condor had built her life. No shifting it. No changing it.

'Of course, Mother. I look forward to seeing you and your necklace.'

Which would be shamelessly displayed around her neck the moment an opportune occasion presented itself. Since it was already mid-November, she didn't have long to wait for the festive season to be in full swing.

Nick set the telephone receiver down and once more stared at the packet on his desk. Part of him wanted to drop it in the litter bin unopened, yet another part of him wanted to know what his father thought he was worth. With a sense of very dark cynicism, he decided it was best to know the finishing line so he could put it completely behind him.

He opened the packet.

It contained two letters.

Predictably enough, one was from a lawyer, Javier Estes, now handling the Ramirez estate. The other, surprisingly, was handwritten by Enrique and addressed very personally to Nick. Its content was stunning in its intimate knowledge of almost every detail of Nick's life and the big punchline at the end of it put a seductively new and challenging spin on his world.

His mind was still intensely engaged with it when his PA opened the door between their offices and his mother made her entrance.

It was always *an entrance*.

Even at fifty-five…looking not a day over thirty-five, if that—she was the ultimate display of female beauty, with a lushly curved body that screamed sexy woman, and she certainly made the most of all she had.

Wherever she went in public, eyes swivelled to look and were instantly trapped into keeping on watching her because she was so very watchable, everything and everyone in her vicinity simply fading into insignificance. Miss Universe was still strutting her stuff with no encroachment whatsoever from the years that had passed since she'd won that title.

Her thick, wonderfully lustrous, long wavy hair looked like a rippling stream of dark brown silk, temptingly touchable. Her large, amber eyes had a hypnotic quality. Whenever she focused them on a man, he seemed to drown in them. Her nose was perfect. Her full-lipped sexy mouth was positively mesmerising, as were the flash of her gleaming white teeth.

And, of course, her long graceful neck was invariably adorned by dazzling jewellery which complemented her dazzling beauty and dazzling, up-to-the-minute, designer clothes. Today she was in black and white with just the right dramatic touches of red.

The moment the door behind her was closed, her hands were reaching out, gesturing for him to give her what she wanted. 'Well…?' It was a prod, delivered with a provocatively appealing smile.

Nick strolled around to the front of his desk and casually propped himself against it, viewing his mother with considerable cynical amusement as he delivered some news that might wilt her monstrous vanity.

'I don't think you're the only woman who received an emerald necklace from Enrique Ramirez this morning.'

Her perfectly smooth brow defied its many Botox treatments and frowned. 'What do you mean?'

'Apparently oats were being sown all around the world in my father's polo-playing years. I have a half-brother in England, and another in the USA, both of whom have impressed my dear dead Dad every bit as much as I have, despite all three of us being his bastard sons. Which undoubtedly means he felt a debt of gratitude to their mothers, as well.'

'Oh!' She shrugged. Her mouth twisted into a wistful smile. 'He really was quite irresistible. I have no doubt any woman would fall for him. But not so good for you, Nick. I guess this means Enrique has cut any inheritance for you three ways.'

The inheritance was irrelevant. Nick wanted to meet his half-brothers. And to do that, he had to fulfil a dead man's crazy fantasy of reliving a different life through his illegitimate son…a life filled with real love and commitment, fidelity and fatherhood. It was either marry and have his wife at least pregnant within the next twelve months, or never learn anything more about his half-brothers.

That was the bare bones of Enrique's wishes…his challenge to Nick.

Forget the rest.

Nick didn't believe in love and marriage and happy families, but he could and would outwardly comply with those terms in order to get to a meeting with his half-brothers—his real blood family however fragmented it was, not step-siblings who came and went with his mother's marriages. He wanted to meet Enrique Ramirez's other by-blows, wanted to know if they were anything like himself, wanted to feel he was not alone.

'There is no inheritance to be had,' he lied, aware that his mother couldn't help herself from plotting for it if he told her the truth. He smiled sardonically as he added, 'My father has graciously granted me some knowledge of a family I went seeking when I was eighteen. What you might call too little, too late.'

'Half-brothers…' The Botox got another workout. 'Are you going to go looking for them now?'

'I don't have any key to finding them. Unlike me they haven't been aware that Enrique fathered them so the Ramirez name would mean nothing to them. I've been told their identities will be revealed to me when the estate is settled. I can wait. In the meantime, I'm going to get on with my business. If you'll leave me to it…'

He strolled over to the door and opened it for her. 'Thank you for your visit. I'm glad you're happy with your necklace.'

'You're not disappointed, Nick?'

He shrugged. 'He who expects nothing cannot be disappointed.'

'Oh, you…' She tapped his cheek in mock exasperation, her golden amber eyes looking for some chink in his cynical armour. 'You should have fought Enrique for some recognition while he was still alive. You've always been too proud, Nick. Too independent.'

'The product of my circumstances. Goodbye, Mother.'

With nothing to get her pretty teeth into, she accepted the exit line, undoubtedly eager now to get the emerald necklace valued to see how much she'd been worth to Enrique Ramirez. His mother was incredibly good at maths when it came to totting up the profit from each connection she'd made.

Left to himself again, Nick concentrated on formulating how best to get to the end he wanted without paying too much for it. He simply didn't have enough information—no names, no descriptions, no ages—to try finding his half-brothers himself. The only guarantee of meeting them was to go down the route Enrique had laid down.

No way was he going to lose out on seeing if he could connect with some *real* family, so that meant he had to face marriage and fatherhood first. The trick was to create a situation he could live with. He didn't want any child of his suffering through divorce, getting screwed up from feeling unwanted. If he had to have a child, he needed to set up a stable environment for it.

His mind kept zapping to one woman.

He'd trust Tess to do right by him—right by their child.

He was almost sure he'd be able to work out an agreement with her—a sensible legal agreement that protected all parties. Tess wasn't like any of the other women he knew—the women who'd jump at marrying him because of who and what he was. Tess didn't want anything from him, didn't want anything from any man.

But she might want a child.

And she knew where Nick was coming from.

Tessa Steele came from the same place.

It didn't matter that she was Brian Steele's daughter—real daughter—she had a mind of her own and had made a life of her own, just like Nick.

The big question was…would she be interested in forging a life in partnership with him, given the incentive of having a child together?

CHAPTER TWO

'THERE'S nothing of you in him, Tessa,' her father growled, a disgruntled look on his face as he studied her two-month-old son.

Nothing of *him*, he meant. Tess knew she was her father's favourite child because he could see his genes in her red hair, fair skin and blue eyes. She'd never been sure if this was a natural hang-up with him— some male primitive need to see the imprint of himself repeated—or a reaction against having another man's child passed off as his. Nick's mother had left a lot of emotional havoc in the wake of her marriage to Brian Steele.

Undoubtedly it had been wounded pride that had driven her father to plunge straight into marriage with another spectacular woman—the blonde and beautiful star of stage and screen, Livvy Curtin. This unlikely coupling had only lasted two years, but at least a child of his own had come out of it and after the divorce had been settled, Livvy had been happy for Brian to have the major share of custody, leaving herself less burdened in pursuing her acting career.

Tess had always known she was loved by her father. Even after his third and still current marriage had produced two sons of whom he was extremely proud, he'd kept a very soft spot for his one and only daughter—a softness which was considerably resented by his third wife who'd taken every opportunity to shunt Tess off to her *real* mother, who much preferred to ignore

that reality. Livvy—*you are not to call me Mummy*—
had no interest whatsoever in even acting out a maternal role.

Tess's own life experience fed her determination to
keep a very simple family line for her child. No marriages. No divorces. No messy extended relationships.
Above all, her son was going to know he was loved
by his mother. And his genetic pattern was irrelevant.
She'd given birth to this baby and he was hers. All
hers.

'He does have curly hair,' she pointed out, though
her own curls were inherited from Livvy, not her father.

Brian Steele's hair was dead straight, like a wire-
brush, and the red was all white now. The blue eyes,
however, hadn't faded one whit with age and were as
sharp as ever as they swung to his daughter, wanting
to pin her down on a few matters which she'd been
successfully evading.

They were sitting in the sunny courtyard at the
Steele family's Singleton property, both of them taking time out from their individual business interests.
This securely secluded country home provided the privacy Tess had wanted for having her baby, and since
this was her father's first grandchild, he'd readily
granted her the occupation of it for a few months while
he and his wife were currently winging between the
Steele family residences in Sydney and Melbourne,
keeping up their social engagements.

'Are you going to tell me who the father is?'

'It doesn't matter who, Dad.' She smiled her own
deep maternal love at the black-haired, green-eyed
baby in the rocker at her feet. 'He's mine.'

And thank God his olive skin was never going to

EMMA DARCY 21

have a problem with being out in the Australian sun.
No rigid restrictions for *his* childhood. No fear of dis-
figuring freckles rammed into him. Her own mother's
brainwashing edict—'You'll turn out ugly, ugly, ugly,
if you don't cover up and wear a big hat'—would
never be a part of his life.

'Tessa, I understand you didn't want to marry the
guy...'

'He wouldn't have wanted to marry me, either,'
tripped off her tongue before she could think better of
revealing that piece of information.

'Why not?' Her father sounded affronted, as though
any man should feel enormously honoured to be her
husband. After all, she was a Steele, daughter of a
billionaire, heiress to a fair chunk of the family mining
fortune, and not without physical attraction when Tess
bothered to play up her natural assets.

She shook her head, not wanting to give away any
clues to the identity of her son's other parent. Her
father would be even more affronted to know it was
Nick Ramirez he could thank for this grandchild.

'Does he even know about your having his child?'

'No. I didn't tell him. Things would only get messy
if I did.'

'Is he already married?'

'No.' Her own vivid blue eyes lasered his. 'It was
just a once only thing, Dad. A big mistake in hindsight. Wrong for both of us. Okay?'

Wrong for Nick, anyway. He'd made that perfectly
clear to her afterwards, showing how appalled he was
at having been caught up in the spontaneous combus-
tion that had ended in wild hot sex with Brian Steele's
daughter.

'Don't you think he might guess when he sees you with a baby?' her father nagged.

'That's very unlikely,' Tess figured that having sex with her was now a sealed compartment in Nick's memory, never to be reopened. 'On the whole, we don't mix socially,' she explained. 'And by the time it's generally known I have a child, the date of birth will be blurred, so there won't be any ready connection to him.'

'You don't *want* him to know,' her father shrewdly concluded.

It was all too complicated, Tess thought. Apart from the family entanglements, on a purely personal level she was not the kind of woman Nick normally chased and bedded, and given his own background, he would absolutely hate the fact of having been involved in an accidental pregnancy. Especially with her!

He was anti-marriage and totally cynical about any *love* relationship lasting. Fatherhood was an extremely sore point with him and if control of his life was taken out of his hands by having fatherhood thrust upon him... Tess mentally shuddered at his possible reaction. Fierce resentment would be the least of it and she was not about to let that touch her son.

Better for Nick that he didn't know. Better for herself, too. Nick Ramirez was like forbidden fruit. She couldn't stop wanting him even though she knew being near him was poisonous to any peace or happiness in her life. It had been like breaking an addiction to give up dealing with him professionally when she could no longer hide her pregnancy. To invite a lifelong tie with him by telling him about their child... Tess knew that could only bring her continuous torment.

'Keeping secrets...' Her father's breath hissed out from between his teeth, a sure sign of unease. 'It's a recipe for future grief. Time will come when the boy will want to know who his father is.' His shaggy white eyebrows beetled down. 'Are you going to tell him lies? Say his father's dead?'

'I don't know. I haven't thought that far ahead.'

'Well, start thinking about it, Tessa,' he sternly advised. 'Best get things straight with the father now because your son has the right to know who he is and shocks aren't good further down the road.'

She looked askance at him, trying to gauge if she dared bring up the sensitive past. Only recently Livvy had told her what had happened all those years ago between her father and Nick. As Brian's new second wife, she'd heard all about *the boy's* visit from her angry husband, how Miss Centre of her own Bloody Universe, Nadia Kilman/Steele/Manning, hadn't bothered to tell her Brazilian lover's bastard son that he wasn't Brian's son.

'Like...with Nick Ramirez, Dad?' she asked hesitantly.

He grimaced at the reminder, then glanced sharply at her. 'Who told you about that?'

'Livvy.'

He snorted. 'No doubt your mother recounted it as a piece of high drama.'

'Actually she thought I should be aware of the family background since I was doing business with him.'

'Business...' His eyes openly mocked that motivation. 'Just a line for Livvy to hang her tittle-tattle onto. Business is business. A man as successful as Nick Ramirez is at what he does, would never let who you are get in the way of what's working for him. Besides, he eventually took his real father's name and you have the right to mine. He'd respect that.'

'But it was a shock to him...back then?' Tess prompted, wanting to continue this thread of their conversation.

'Hell of a shock!' Her father winced over the memory. 'I didn't deal kindly with him. Something I'll always regret. I was so mad at Nadia, so mad at being tricked into thinking he was my son, I took it out on him. And none of it was his fault. He was just a boy, fighting for what he believed was his rights.'

'So in a way...you admired him?' she probed.

A wry laugh. 'No, I hated his guts because I kept seeing that blasted Brazilian popinjay in him. But afterwards I felt ashamed of how I broke the truth to him. I was furious with Nadia at not having done it herself.' A rueful sigh. 'He was only seven years old yet he stood his ground, defying me until I smashed his belief in me as his father. And then...it was like I'd killed something in him.'

He shook his head at her. 'I wouldn't like you to put your son—my grandchild—in that kind of position, Tessa. I don't care about the father. Just don't do it to your boy. He has the right to know. Know from the very beginning.'

It was a sobering piece of advice, cutting through the emotional turmoil that always swirled around Tess's thinking about Nick. To her it was totally unforgettable that he'd been *embarrassed* about having sex with her, that he couldn't put it behind him fast enough, careful never to even slightly refer to it after they'd agreed that one intimate flashpoint shouldn't affect their work relationship.

He frequently used her services as a casting agent

to get the right people acting in the TV commercials he created. In the months of face to face business discussions with him during the early stages of her pregnancy, Tess had waited for—yearned for—some sign that he might feel drawn towards having more than a work relationship with her.

A stupid wish, she knew. And, of course, no sign had come. In fact, it hadn't taken him long to start a hot affair with another one of the models who streamed through his life. And bed.

Once Livvy had told her the background, Tess had realised that Nick Ramirez would never seek an intimate connection with Brian Steele's daughter. It had probably amused him to use *her* casting agency, although after she'd proved her worth to his business, he'd come to respect her judgement.

They'd even reached a kind of platonic friendship in their mutual understanding of each other's backgrounds. But the desire that had flared up one night…to Nick it had been highly *undesirable* in hindsight, never to be allowed to slip past his guard again.

Common sense had forced her to adopt the same attitude whenever they'd met professionally, and each meeting had hammered home the point he wanted no consequences from what he obviously considered a moment of madness. Business, as before, was strictly adhered to.

However, Tess now realised her father was right. Her own feelings and Nick's feelings were irrelevant. It wasn't their baby's fault that he was *a consequence*. They'd made a child and every child had the right to know its biological parents. She was going to have to tell Nick, but not until she was feeling less raw about it, more able to adopt and hold onto a totally convincing independent stance.

Her mobile phone played its call tune.

She smiled at her father as she picked up the personal communicator and stood to move away for some privacy. 'Keep an eye on Zack for me while I deal with this?'

He nodded while grumbling, 'Don't know why you had to call him Zack. What kind of name is that? Some fancy idea from your mother, I'll bet...'

This was undoubtedly her father's way of letting her know he was well aware of the media's spotlight on her mother's arrival in Sydney yesterday, and he was assuming the call was from Livvy who had recently earned his disapproval by attaching herself to a toy-boy.

Tess had made the same assumption which was why she was moving out of earshot, knowing that any conversation with her mother would draw an acid side commentary from her father. She was already opening the gate out of the enclosed courtyard as she accepted the call and identified herself.

'Tess, it's Nick. Nick Ramirez.'

The shock of hearing so directly from the man who'd just been the focus of considerable mental and emotional conflict, robbed Tess of any ready reply. It also jolted her feet into a dead halt until she recovered sense enough to realise she didn't want this conversation overheard, either.

'Where are you right now?' Nick ran on, apparently too impatient to wait for a normal greeting.

Facing the polo field where your father played with my father, setting off the train of events which has led to the situation we now have between us.

Tess checked the wild drift of her mind and the headlong rush of her feet to wide open spaces, took a deep breath, and with as calm a voice as she could manage, asked, 'What is the problem, Nick?'

It had to be something to do with the casting agency. Had her personal assistant messed up *his* business in some critical way?

'There's no problem,' he hastily assured her.

'Then why are you calling me?'

'I want to meet with you.'

'What for?'

Silence.

A wave of electric fear shot through every nerve in Tess's body, leaving them at rigid attention. Had he somehow heard about the baby? Did he think he might be the father?

'Can we get together for lunch?' he pressed. 'You must be back in Sydney. Livvy's here.'

'No, I'm not in Sydney, Nick.'

'Didn't you tell me your mother needed you with her as a people manager while she directed her first movie? Wasn't that why I've had to deal through your PA and not with you personally for the past six months? Because you were away with your mother?'

'Yes,' Tess acknowledged, her stomach contracting as she realised how easily Nick could uncover her lies if he put his mind to it.

'Well, Livvy flew in from LA yesterday,' he went on. 'Since you're answering this call, you're obviously back in Australia, as well. So where are you now?'

'I'm at Singleton, visiting with my father.' That, at least, was the truth, and no way in the world would Nick Ramirez front up here.

His sigh seethed with frustration. 'Tess, I need to get together with you.'

The driving purpose in his voice sent a quiver through her heart. 'What for, Nick?'

He ignored the question, seizing on an event where her presence was certainly expected. 'The premiere of *Waking Up* next Thursday night...'

It was a teen horror movie, its release timed for the end of the school year, hoping to draw big audiences once the Christmas vacation started. Tess had planned to return to Sydney tomorrow, settle back into her home at Randwick, catch up with her mother, buy something suitable to wear to the premiere...

'I remember you did the casting for that movie,' Nick said with considerable satisfaction in having connected her to a definite time and place. 'If you don't have an escort lined up for the red carpet, I'll fill in. Okay?'

Shocked by what could not, by any stretch of the imagination, be called a *business* arrangement, Tess could not contain her astonishment at this suggestion. 'Why?' tripped straight off her tongue.

'Why not?' came shooting back at her. 'Have you finally found a guy you care about? A guy who'd object to your being with me?'

The terse tone of his voice implied he didn't care for any such hitch in his plans. Tess was goaded into saying, 'Isn't there a woman hanging around your neck who'd object to me sharing a premiere spotlight with you?'

'Not a factor,' he claimed.

'I can't believe you don't have someone on your string.'

'That string will be cut before next Thursday.'

An emphatically decisive note there.

Tess wondered if it was an ominous note for her. It wasn't unusual for women to come and go very quickly in Nick's life, but linking the current lady's exit to this out-of-character public date with her...was Nick wiping his slate clean to deal with fatherhood?

This meeting could not be about business. Yet how could he know about the baby when she had literally dropped out of circulation in Sydney before her pregnancy showed?

She took a deep breath and confronted the issue. 'What's this about, Nick?'

'I'll tell you when I see you, Tess. Where and when do I pick you up for the premiere?'

He was arrogantly assuming she didn't have an escort lined up. Or she'd just mentally jettisoned any prior arrangement to be with him instead. Fair enough, she supposed, given his belief that she'd been in Los Angeles for the past six months and definitely not deeply engaged with any hometown guy. Nick Ramirez was an important client who did warrant some indulgence and he was demanding it.

Besides, with her father's very recent advice still weighing heavily on her mind, this was clearly an opportunity for her to get personal with Nick on her son's behalf, if the circumstances felt reasonably favourable. Better not to protest too much when she had her own agenda. And no man in tow, anyway.

On the other hand, until such time as she felt right about telling him of their child, she didn't want Nick seeing Zack, or even knowing about him.

'I'll be staying at The Regent Hotel that night.' Completely neutral ground. 'The after-show party is to be held there,' she went on. 'I'm not sure when the limousines will start rolling to the theatre...'

'Meet me in the lobby of the hotel for drinks at six.'

A public place was fine. 'Okay. Six it is.'

'Thanks, Tess.'

Was that a tinge of relief in his voice? Tess was intrigued by the idea of Nick Ramirez needing her for something personal.

'You know, I've actually missed you while you've been away,' he added, and she could hear him smiling through the words, the dry mocking smile he attached to any expression of emotion. 'I look forward to being with you, Tess.'

Connection cut.

She stood in stunned stillness.

This call couldn't possibly have been related to any suspicion she'd had a baby—*his* baby. Clearly Nick still believed her LA cover story which explained her lengthy absence from normal business. The most curious and nerve-tingling part was...his saying that he'd missed her, which had to mean *her, the person,* because this movie premiere had nothing to do with business and he had offered her his arm for it.

In the context of his previous strongly negative attitude towards any personal involvement with her, this didn't make sense.

None of it made sense.

He hadn't even said goodbye to his current girlfriend yet.

The only possible answer was... Nick Ramirez wanted something from her—something urgently needed by him—something important enough to drive him into breaking his own rules to get it.

Which put a fascinating spin on this extraordinary move.

Tess decided she had nothing to fear from it.

And quite possibly much to gain.

CHAPTER THREE

NICK was smiling to himself as he entered The Regent Hotel. Brilliant move—starting off a serious personal relationship with Tess in the publicity blaze of a premiere. If Enrique's surveillance guy was on the job, reporting back to Javier Estes, he could hardly miss it.

Step one towards *love and marriage.*

Six o'clock and the lobby was abuzz with people coming in from the day, making plans for the night, waiting to be joined by others before proceeding elsewhere. Nick knew the bank of elevators was at the back of the open lounge area and he took up a position in a relatively clear space near the reception counter so Tess could easily spot him when she came down from her room. Any minute now. Unlike most women he knew, Tess had always been a stickler for punctuality.

No doubt time-keeping had been drilled into her at boarding school where bells were invariably rung to command a move from one place to another and punishments were handed out for dallying beyond an acceptable limit. It was another part of their background in common...boarding school, where many inconvenient children got dumped. It was also one thing he was sure Tess would agree on—no boarding school for their child *if* they had one.

Nick was not yet fully committed to the idea of being a father, taking on the heavy and enduring responsibility it entailed. At this point he was only playing with the factors, seeing if they could be moved into an acceptable framework. He could envisage doing the marriage part of the mission with Tess. That was mostly paperwork—a contract signed and subsequently dissolved at the parties' convenience. The child part was far more troubling.

Weirdly enough, Enrique's challenge on the fatherhood issue had certainly stirred him up on how parents should treat their children. Nick found himself brooding over an endless list of negatives coming straight out of his own life. But to carry through the positives that every child deserved was by no means an easy task. It would require some very solid planning.

If he went through with this.

It was a damnedly insidious challenge Enrique had thrown out. To get to brothers of his own, he had to beget a child of his own. But a child was a child, with much to be done for him or her. The brothers he didn't know yet had to be adults if they'd been conceived and born during Enrique's international polo-playing days—men he might not even like, let alone care about, not worth going through all this to get to them.

Nevertheless, having them arbitrarily withheld from him...

That was intolerable!

The sound buzz in the lobby changed—surprise and excited speculation lilting through it—alerting him to people turning, looking up to the head of the grand staircase which led down from the mezzanine level where the main restaurant was situated. Bound to be one of the actors starring in tonight's premiere, Nick thought, his gaze flashing up in the expectation of seeing an instantly recognisable face.

Recognition certainly hit him but for a few stunned

moments Nick couldn't quite come to grips with what he was seeing.

Tess…walking down the stairs like a movie queen?

Tess…looking so fabulous, so glowingly exquisite, she would leave both *her* mother and *his* in the shade, even on their best-foot-forward days!

Her red hair, shining with golden highlights, rippled down in long loose curls all over and around her pale pearly shoulders. Framed by this spectacular halo and with the natural prettiness of her features enhanced by artistically applied make-up, her face positively sparkled with star-power, vividly lit by her bright blue eyes and even brighter white smile.

She wore a dress that would have been a show-stopper on any red carpet in the world. Silvery beaded mauve lace barely cupped her breasts, the low decolletage caught together by swathes of mauve chiffon, hugging her small waist and tied tightly with long silver tassels that swayed over a long skirt of rows of lace and seductive frills, graduating in shades of mauve to smoky grey and deep violet. The frills played peek-a-boo with her long shapely legs and feet encased in very high-heeled sexy silver sandals.

Complementing this was the jewellery—diamond bracelet, long dangly diamond earrings and around her neck a fine chain of diamonds leading to a whopping big diamond pendant. The heiress to a mining fortune was certainly not hiding her light under any bushel tonight!

This vision of Tess did odd things to Nick's stomach.

And predictable things to his groin.

Which completely fused his thought processes.

*   *   *

Tess paused halfway down the staircase. She'd spotted Nick before starting this perilous descent on the sexy stilettos that had to be worn with this dress. His focus had been trained elsewhere but it certainly had a fix on her now. He was staring straight at her. But he wasn't moving, wasn't taking one step to meet her.

Tess felt an almost evil satisfaction at the stunned look on his face. Just because she'd made a point of not dressing up for him all during their professional relationship, not wanting to be viewed as another one of the herd of women dying to draw his attention, it didn't mean she couldn't lay out the bait with the best of them when she wanted to. All it took was time; time with a hair stylist, time with a beautician, time shopping. And money, of course. The old adage—fine feathers made fine birds...always held true.

If she had to rock the boat between them by telling him about their child, she'd decided she might as well rock the boat in every direction—force him to see her as not so *accidentally* desirable, make him remember how he'd felt with her the night Zack had been conceived. She wasn't sure if it was reckless pride driving her into being deliberately provocative or a savagely primitive need to knock Nick's socks off so he'd reassess what he wanted from their relationship.

It was almost a year since he'd walked away from that explosive night of wild careless sex, forcing her to set it aside, as well. Was he remembering it now? Was that why he wasn't moving to meet her? Bad Tess, stirring it up for him! Out of control Tess, not doing the sensible thing for once.

A fierce rebellion was surging against the pigeonhole Nick had put her into. He was still standing flatfooted in the reception area, not coming to her. Fine!

She'd go all the way to him, force him to acknowledge he was with her tonight. At his own insistence!

She resumed her descent of the staircase, a burning anger turning her previous graceful carriage into a flaunting strut. Perhaps a sense of courtesy finally kicked through Nick's shock. He started towards the foot of the staircase, and, as was usual with him, people rolled back from his path like the Red Sea for Moses.

He had the commanding charisma of being spectacularly tall, dark and handsome, especially in formal clothes, and there was something about his Latin-lover looks that stirred a spine-tingling sense of danger, adding immeasurably to the sexual allure of the man.

When Tess had first laid eyes on him, she'd thought there wouldn't be a woman in the world who'd be immune to at least a fleeting desire to sample him in bed. The trouble was Nick knew it, and something in her had instantly wanted to be the exception, defying his power to get women virtually dropping at his feet.

But she was no exception.

She'd fallen when he'd opened the door to having sex with her. And she'd fall again, given the chance. Without a doubt, it would be much, much easier to tell Nick he was the father of her child if he was sharing a bed with her.

However, if she had lit any fire in him just now, he certainly had it under control by the time he met her at the foot of the stairs, halting her on the step above him by taking her hand and lifting it to his mouth in mocking homage.

'Pure Hollywood, Tess,' he purred through a sensuous brushing of his lips over her skin. Then he gave his twisted little smile and cocked a sardonic eyebrow. 'Getting into the spirit of a premiere?'

Electric tingles ran up her arm and shot adrenaline through her bloodstream, sharpening her mind to defence stations as her all too vulnerable heart pitter-pattered its distress at the dying hope for anything different coming from Nick. If he wanted something personal from her tonight, it was obviously not going to comprise a shift away from platonic friendship.

'I thought I'd better lift my game for the publicity limelight,' she explained, colouring all her efforts to *affect* him as something professional, not personal.

His laugh was tinged with irony. 'You didn't just lift it, Tess. You've totally outclassed any possible competition.'

'I'm not competing,' she swiftly denied, hating the thought that he suspected she might be. 'Have I overdone it? Is that why you just stood there and stared instead of coming to greet me?'

He shook his head, eyes twinkling amusement at the sudden crack in her confidence. 'You haven't overdone it, Tess. In fact, you deserve a standing ovation for a perfect production. I just wasn't expecting the grand entrance from you.'

She shrugged. 'Well, I can be my mother's daughter when I choose to be. And why not when I'm going to a premiere?'

'Why not, indeed? I simply needed a moment or two to get accustomed to *this* image of you.'

'You have seen me dressed up before,' shot out of her mouth, propelled by a rampaging need for him to acknowledge he had found her desirable the last time she'd fine-feathered herself—the night they had both attended a product launch party. Separately. And ended up intimately together.

The thick black lashes lowered, instantly veiling *his* response to the memory. His full-lipped provocative mouth moved into a teasing moue. 'Playing with fire, Tess?'

Heat whooshed up her neck and into her cheeks and she silently and violently cursed the fair translucent skin which was such a telltale barometer of her feelings. Her inner agitation seized on a counter-attack to defend herself.

'You're the one crossing the line, Nick. I didn't ask you to be with me tonight. You asked yourself, remember?'

'I did,' he agreed, but his mouth was still taunting, turning her into just another woman who fancied getting into his trousers.

'As for the *grand entrance*, you triggered that yourself,' she ran on, her fight to equalise everything gathering a fierce momentum. 'Firstly you were so stuck in a world of your own I couldn't draw your attention from the mezzanine level. Then when I started down to collect you and you did happen to look up, instead of bounding up the stairs to meet me, you stand and stare, making me come all the way down...'

'Don't tell me you didn't enjoy creating a sensation, Tess,' he slid in mockingly.

'I happen to be dressed for the occasion, Nick Ramirez, and instead of puffing up your macho ego, thinking I've done it to impress you, perhaps you'll now escort me back upstairs so we can have a bite to eat in the coffee shop before we leave for the theatre.'

'At your service.' He flashed her an openly charming grin as he took the hand he was still holding, tucked it around his arm and stepped up to do her bidding. 'And that tart tongue of yours has just reminded me why I've missed you so much.'

'Too much honey for the busy bee?' she slung at him. Her heartbeat was in major overdrive, causing her mind to zing beyond the bounds of discretion. She was viciously jealous of all his other women, but showing it with her tart tongue was not a good idea.

To her intense relief he laughed, his wicked green eyes dancing pleasure in her, and the steely pride Tess was trying to keep in her spine was in instant danger of melting. It wasn't fair that one man should be so attractive. If it was only the physical impact, it wouldn't be so difficult to set it at a distance and ignore it. But when his mind clicked with hers, which it did all too frequently on many levels, everything within her yearned to have Nick Ramirez as *her man*.

Unfortunately, knowing that was never going to happen did not diminish the desire. Tess mostly managed to counter it by being as sane and down-to-earth as she could be around Nick. She just wasn't on top of that game tonight. Probably never would be again. The six-month break from frequent practice at it left her feeling inept, and the sense that everything had to change between them anyway eroded the old need to keep it up.

Returning to the sore point of his women, Tess decided she might as well be blunt in sorting out this current situation. Pitching her voice to a light bantering tone, she invited him to be forthcoming. 'So tell me why you dumped your current bedmate to come out with me tonight.'

He shrugged. 'Purely an incidental. She was ready

to move on.' A sardonic twist of his mouth as he added, 'Had another guy already lined up.'

'Having realised *you* weren't ever going to put a ring on her finger?'

'I never lead any woman to believe that, Tess.'

'Doesn't stop them from hoping for it. After all, it's part of the deal.'

'What deal?'

'You know perfectly well *what deal*. It's part and parcel of the high-flying world we were both born into. *Men go after the most attractive women they can afford; women go after the richest men they can attract.*'

Her father and his mother were prime examples of this pattern of behaviour.

'I don't buy my women,' Nick protested.

She flicked him a mocking look. 'Yes, you do. You buy them with who and what you are. You just never close the deal. They don't realise at first that you're only into visiting their bedrooms, not staying there. I bet every one of them thinks she'll be the one to keep you at her side.'

'Well, I can't control hopes but I certainly don't ever feed them.'

'Maintaining your brand of integrity?'

'I have always hated deceit, Tess.'

Which set all her nerves on edge over what she'd been keeping from him. Maybe she should blurt it out right now, throw fatherhood into his lap and watch how he dealt with it. On the other hand, he hadn't yet laid out his purpose behind being her escort tonight and there had to be one. Tess didn't believe he'd simply been *missing her tart tongue*.

The fatherhood issue could wait a bit longer.

She wanted her curiosity satisfied first.

'Will a plate of fruit and cheese do it for you or do you want something more substantial?' Nick asked matter-of-factly as he steered her to a vacant padded booth in the coffee shop overlooking the lobby. 'And what would you like to drink?'

'Hmmm...a lovely rich creamy Brandy Alexander to drink and a wicked slice of Chocolate Mud cake to eat,' she rolled out with sinful relish, deciding comfort food could be forgiven tonight since she was feeling distinctly fraught. 'And I won't share, so if you're hungry, too, order something for yourself.'

At his look of surprise at her grossly non-dieting order, she dryly pointed out, 'You are not with a fig-ure-watching model tonight and I feel like spoiling myself.'

His grin was warm this time. 'Curves are good.' His gaze dropped to her cleavage as he saw her seated, causing her wretched skin to flush again. Then to fluster her further, there was definitely a lustful simmer in his eyes when they smiled into hers. 'I'll go and order, organise quick service. Be back in a minute.'

She nodded, telling herself she was dressed to at-tract that kind of male response and Nick had just given it to her. Being the man he was, he probably couldn't help himself. She should feel happy about it. She wanted him to want her. But not just because her rather full breasts were being flaunted tonight. That put her in the same category as all his other women.

Tess shook her head, hopelessly confused over what she wanted from tonight with Nick. She certainly didn't want him to see how vulnerable she was to the desires he stirred. It was lucky there were beads sewn over the lace of the skimpy bodice, hiding the fact that her nipples had just become embarrassingly hard and prominent.

Really, it was highly vexing to get so messed up in a sexual sense when she wasn't getting any answers from him. Plenty of reaction to her but no reasons for his own actions. She took a few deep breaths to cool herself down, resolved to take some initiative in questioning him when he returned, and wished life could be a lot easier to figure out.

Before she could formulate a line of attack, Nick was sliding onto the seat on the other side of their table, positioning himself directly opposite her, lining up a face to face conversation, which he immediately started.

'Where do you fit into the deal, Tess?'

She looked blankly at him. 'What deal are you talking about?'

'The one where men go after the most attractive women they can afford, and women go after the richest men they can attract.'

'I don't fit.' She shrugged. 'I guess you can't separate an heiress from the fortune that comes with her. As a marriage prospect, men would inevitably be thinking more about my money than me, and I'd rather not feel they were with me because of it.'

'Is that why you remain single, Tess? You don't trust a guy to love you for the person you are?'

She frowned at him. 'Why are you trying to psychoanalyse me again? You're not very good at it, Nick. Last time you decided I'd been ripped off and hurt by so many guys I'd become an ice maiden. All because I wasn't playing your game.'

'My game?'

'Where you put out a blast of sexual magnetism and

I'm supposed to turn into putty so you can squeeze me however you want.'

He rolled his eyes at her description of his modus operandi with women. 'I did not try to blast you with sexual magnetism.'

'No, in all fairness, it probably flows naturally from you. But you were peeved at my resistance to it. Why else would you cast me in ice?'

'You were also denying your femininity, Tess,' he pointed out. 'Always wearing androgynous jeans, shirts, no make-up, hair scraped back in an unflattering style…'

'I was simply going about my business which does not require me to impress anyone with my looks. As a casting agent, it's the looks of my clients that I peddle. Better that I don't distract from them.'

'Okay, so I read you wrong.' His mouth twitched into that sexy moue again. 'And you proved me wrong. It's been a long time now since I attached ice to your sexuality.'

'That was only a year ago,' she reminded him, the date being extremely pertinent to her, considering she still had to tell him about Zack.

'I know you better now,' he pressed on.

'Intimately better,' she pushed, recklessly intent on forcing him to remember what she couldn't forget. Especially when the result of their intimacy had to be revealed.

'Any objection to us getting that close again, Tess?'

It came out of nowhere.

No foreplay.

No seductive moves suggesting it might be on offer.

Just laying sex with him on the table for her to pick up or not as she pleased.

It took Tess's breath away, rendering her totally speechless. Not that her shocked mind was in any kind of working order to formulate thoughts which could be put into words. In fact, its emptiness seemed to be ringing with the echo of her thumping heart.

A waiter arrived at their table and proceeded to serve their drinks and her chocolate cake.

A timely distraction.

Nick couldn't expect her to answer him until they were alone again. He sat back...waiting. Watching her and waiting. And Tess had the weird sense of him harnessing all his dynamic energy, ready to roll right over her reply and get what he wanted any way he could.

But for what purpose?

And why *now*?

CHAPTER FOUR

NICK wondered if he should dump the sexual approach. There was no doubting Tess's shock. She hadn't been expecting it and quite possibly was recoiling from it.

He'd read her provocative strut down the staircase as being aimed at him, a deliberate sexual stir, but maybe she'd simply been doing the female thing of putting on a show, doing it because she could, revelling in being the centre of admiring and amazed attention. Her six months in Hollywood with her mother might well have made this behaviour seem absolutely normal.

Problem was…he had been stirred by it.

Stirred into a highly vivid memory of how it had felt to have nothing between them except the heat of intense and passionate pleasure. Big mistake to ever get sexually involved with a highly useful business connection, he'd told himself, but the truth was…he'd felt himself shifting onto dangerous ground with Tessa Steele and his survival instincts had screamed at him to get out fast—get out and don't revisit that scene. It raised too many ripples of consequence and he didn't want to face any of them.

Now…well, marriage was something else.

And if he was going to have a child with Tess, consequences had to be faced.

He saw having great sex with her as a bonus, and a means of persuading her into considering marriage with him. There was no denying the chemistry between them could be explosive, given free rein. Seeing her dressed to kill tonight, he'd thought she was inviting him to revisit that scene, which could have provided a smooth path into a long intimate relationship with her.

It still could, Nick reasoned, if he played his cards right. He wanted the intimacy with her. In fact, he wanted it so badly the desire was surprisingly uncomfortable.

Tess was sitting very still while the waiter unloaded his tray, setting everything out correctly on the table. Still, silent, tense, her gaze fixed on the guy's hands. Once the waiter had gone, she stared at the cake, finally picking up her fork and carving a slice of it, working the heavy chocolate mixture onto the silver prongs to lift it to her mouth. When it was arranged to her satisfaction, she lifted her gaze and directed a sharp blast of killer blue eyes right at him. It was a look designed to pin him to the wall and make him squirm.

'This doesn't make sense, Nick. Why would you suddenly fancy having another one night stand with me?'

'The experience lives in my memory as one that bears repetition, Tess.'

Hot colour rushed into her cheeks but the laser burn of her eyes did not waver from his. 'I thought you were committed to an easy come, easy go, mindset.'

'Well, that is the most sensible attitude in today's world of changing partners. Less grief all around.'

'Then we should be *gone* as an item. Why come back for seconds?'

'I don't have a one night stand in mind, this time around.'

'I think you'd better lay out what you do have in mind, Nick, because I am feeling distinctly lost on the road you've just taken.'

She shoved the chocolate cake into her mouth, leaving him to talk without any interruption from her. Her gaze was still trained on his face, eyes guarded, yet intensely watchful for every variation of expression from him.

'If we had a much closer relationship, at least you'd know it had nothing to do with your money,' he started slowly, feeling his way forward with careful respect for her feelings. 'In fact, nothing would induce me to touch a cent of the Steele fortune.'

A derisive little laugh gurgled from her throat. 'I thought that applied to me, too.'

He frowned, not understanding. 'What do you mean?'

'Well, after our unplanned...fling...you couldn't drop me fast enough. Didn't want to touch me again. It seemed to me you were appalled to find yourself *in flagrante* with Brian Steele's daughter.'

'You think I care who your father is?' He was astounded she should think it, incensed at the idea that any judgement of her would be based on her parentage. 'Fathers are totally irrelevant to me, Tess. We make our own lives, regardless of them.'

'Irrelevant...' she echoed, as though weighing that concept in her mind. She heaved a deep sigh and gestured with her fork for him to continue before digging it back into the mud cake. 'Okay, I accept that my money is no attraction to you...and you tell me you don't care who my father is, even though you once thought he was yours and got horribly rejected by him...'

'That's ancient history, Tess.'

'Is it, Nick?' She gave him an ironic look. 'I've always thought we are the sum of our past. It's all inside us, driving who and what we are. Take fathers, for instance. I happen to love mine...'

'It's fine that you do,' he swiftly assured her. 'I have no problem with Brian Steele. He had every right to deny I was his son. It was the truth. And I have no problem with you being his daughter.'

It rather amused him that his erstwhile father would end up his father-in-law if Tess married him, and Brian Steele wouldn't be able to deny that their child was his grandchild.

She shook her head, took a deep breath and said, 'Let me get this straight. The only reason that our one night stand was a one night stand for you was because we were doing business together on an ongoing basis, so it wasn't a good idea to extend it into an affair, which might have made things messy between us. Is that right, Nick?'

'Yes.'

Though the main reason had been the strong sense of falling down the same slavish pit his mother's men fell into, losing control of themselves and their lives by giving in to her sexual power over them. Just one night with Tess had demonstrated how addictive she could be—experiencing the whole package of her— and Nick instinctively shied from ceding that control to any woman. However, if he could keep things reasonable, and Tess was a very reasonable woman...

'But since my agency has done business with you...during my absence...for the past six months...'

she went on, building a line of logic, '...you've reap-praised the situation and decided you *can* have a harm-less little affair with me. Is that where we are now, Nick?'

The incredulous note in her voice was warning enough that she'd find his proposal completely off the wall, but it had to be put on the table and the sooner it was done now, the better, giving him a platform to move forward with her.

'Not an affair, Tess. I was thinking more along the lines of us getting married. Having a child together.'

For Tess, it was like a huge shift in the fabric of her life. To say she was thunderstruck was putting it mildly. A hysterical bubble raced around her zapped brain, yelling out *we've already had a child together*. But the big incredible door of *marriage* kept blocking the wild bubble from breaking out into speech.

For the past few minutes she had been see-sawing over spilling the fact of his fatherhood. Several times she had thought the right moment had come, only to be diverted by the seductive idea of Nick positively wanting an affair with her, not just playing with the thought, actually putting it to her, which was amazing enough...

But marriage!

Marriage meant Nick would be her husband, her man, the impossible dream come true...

Except he wasn't saying she was the love of his life—which would be a totally absurd statement any-way, given their recent history. It was eleven months too late to be bringing up any feeling of deep attach-ment to her. No credibility at all. The fantasy of the black prince miraculously becoming her white knight in shining armour simply didn't play out in these circumstances.

In fact, the only thing he was hanging this proposal on seemed to be his desire for a repetition of his sexual experience with her, and since when did marriage have anything to do with his pursuit of bedding a woman?

Which left...*having a child together.*

Setting aside the fact they already had a child together, why would Nick suddenly want the commitment of fatherhood? Here was a man who avoided any long-term relationship commitment like the plague. What had changed his mind?

He hadn't said anything about why he wanted her to be his wife or why he wanted a wife at all! He'd always shown contempt for the institution of marriage, calling it a property trap that only fools would enter of their own free will.

She suddenly remembered he'd just assured her he wouldn't touch a cent of the Steele fortune. And, of course, being the heiress she was, he'd assume she wouldn't bother milking him of *his* assets if it came to a divorce between them. So the property trap wouldn't apply to them if they married. He'd obviously thought that through. But it didn't answer the big question...*why marry her at all?*

'This is...a surprise,' she said rather limply, needing him to bolster the idea with cogent reasons.

'Not an unpleasant one, I hope.' His magnetic smile flashed out, designed to pull her his way. His dark eyes twinkled warm confidence in their reaching a mutual and beneficial understanding. 'I think we could deal very well together, Tess.'

The persuasive purr of his voice was like a siren song, seductively calling her to set obstacles aside and just go with him, whatever he wanted, because she wanted it, too. But a bank of past hurts wouldn't let Tess plunge blindly into what would most certainly be an emotional minefield for her.

'Are you tired of tom-catting around, Nick?'

She set down the cake fork and picked up her drink, eyeing him over the rim of her glass as he constructed an acceptable reply.

'I think monogamy with the right woman could be very comfortable.'

'Mmmh...'

Tess sipped the brandy and cream, trying not to bridle with pleasure at being labelled *the right woman*. This had to be cynical flattery, she told herself. *Comfortable* was far more apt.

Her own pride had forced her into allowing him to *comfortably* continue their professional relationship after their one intimate night together, not creating any emotional drama when he'd moved on to satisfy himself sexually with another woman. But if he thought she'd continue a marriage through one infidelity after another, he could kiss any idea of that comfort zone goodbye!

'You're actually willing to try it,' she posed, gearing up to test his sincerity. '...staying wed to your wife, cleaving only to her until death do you part?'

He grimaced. 'I'm talking about a partnership, Tess, not a life sentence. Like any partnership, as long as it's working for us, fine. If it doesn't give us what we want, then we dissolve it.'

In short, he would act to suit himself. As always. Definitely no declaration of undying love coming from the lips of Nick Ramirez! They were great for kissing, great for promising the most incredible sexual pleasure and satisfaction. But love to last a lifetime? Forget it!

'Didn't you tell me two years was the maximum limit for passion?' She gave him a mocking little smile. 'Even if you've worked up a head of steam for me while I've been absent from your life, do you see us staying married for a longer period?'

He nodded.

She couldn't believe it.

Nick Ramirez offering her a commitment that went beyond the heat of sex?

'That's where the comfort part kicks in,' he explained. 'I've always enjoyed your company, Tess. I never feel bored by you and you've never given off bored vibrations with me. I don't see that changing. Do you?'

'I don't know. Our rather infrequent meetings don't exactly test that assumption, Nick. I'm amazed you're prepared to base a marriage on it. Amazed you've got marriage on your mind at all.' She arched one eyebrow in quizzical challenge. 'Want to tell me why?'

The shutters came down so fast on all his charged-up dynamic energy Tess could almost hear the clanging of steel doors closing out any possible entry to whatever was driving his mind, almost see the signs flashing up—

PRIVATE
TOP SECRET
CLASSIFIED INFORMATION

Tess suspected that Nick Ramirez would never let any woman past the barriers surrounding his heart and soul and he wasn't about to let a wife, either. But one thing she now understood very clearly. The motivation for this marriage proposal went deep and was very personal because Nick was intent on shielding it from her. For some reason he needed a wife and he'd chosen her as the most suitable candidate.

Tess—whose sex appeal had not been completely worn out on their one night stand.

Tess—who hadn't ranted and raved about his moving on from her to the next woman who took his eye.

Tess—who wouldn't take him down financially when it came time to part because she had money to burn herself.

Eminently sensible Tess who wouldn't give him too much grief once his private purpose had been served.

A fast building wave of fierce resentments swelled through her as she waited for Nick to construct a reply aimed at winning her acquiescence to his plan.

No way, she thought venomously. No way in the world was she going to be his bunny in some agenda that held no real caring for her. She was right on edge, ready to explode with a host of blistering home-truths, her nerves jumping so much her skin felt as though it was crawling as she watched him regather himself. No smile. Deadly serious. Dark green eyes locked onto hers, intensely purposeful.

'It's about having a child,' he said softly. 'It's about bringing up our child in a far more stable home than *we* were ever given. You'd be with me on that, wouldn't you, Tess? We know what it was like for us so…' The intensity in his eyes moved up a notch. '…we'd make it different. Better.'

Her heart lodged in her burning throat, choking off the tirade she'd been about to hurl at him.

He knew about Zack.

Had to.

And he'd just been cobbling together a marriage proposal because he felt it was the right thing for their child to have both parents living under the same roof, making a home...

'I think we could make a good go of it together,' he pressed.

Her mind whirled wildly around this contention. She simply hadn't expected Nick to embrace father-hood at all, let alone take the old-fashioned honourable route of actually marrying her for the sake of their child. A horribly cynical voice in the back of her head observed that it was far too late to propose an abortion. Their son was already born. A real flesh-and-blood person. Nick's flesh and blood as well as hers. Had this fact stirred some proprietorial instinct in him?

'You don't have to marry me,' she blurted out, hat-ing the thought of any intimate link between them based on a sense of entrapment. 'I won't mind sharing Zack with you. I'm glad you want to play a part in his life.'

'Zack?' Nick frowned heavily at her.

Gearing up to criticise her choice of name, just like her father, Tess thought. 'I don't see that you have any rights over our son as yet, Nick,' she stated somewhat belligerently. 'You weren't around when I gave birth to him two months ago, so...'

'You gave birth...to our son...two months ago?'

His voice climbed from a grated growl to a powerful punch of seething emotions. His eyes blazed with frightening intensity. His whole face tightened as though throwing up a wall of resistance to what she'd just told him. His shoulders squared into fighting rigidity.

The snap of breaking glass drew Tess's gaze down. The V-shaped goblet that had held Nick's martini was lying askew on the table, its fine stem still gripped upright in his hand. His hand was cut, oozing drops of blood.

Flesh-and-blood reality, Tess thought, her own heart thumping wildly at having faced Nick with it.

This was different to making a plan.

Different to putting forward a proposal.

Zack…their child…was real.

Right now real.

And Nick had not known about him!

The realisation of what she'd just done hit Tess like a knock-out blow.

She shut her eyes.

She shut her mouth.

Everything had just crashed out of control.

She had comprehensively lost the plot.

CHAPTER FIVE

IT WASN'T a lie.

As much as Nick wanted it to be—needed it to be—logic kept ramming it through the savagely defensive resistance in his mind that what Tess had just revealed *could not be* a lie. She had unwittingly spilled the truth, thinking he already knew it.

There had been no artfulness in what she'd said, no intent to get anything out of him, no reason at all for her to lie about having had his child. And the appalled look on her face when she'd realised his marriage proposal had not been about the baby she had secretly kept from him…impossible to even think she'd made a mistake and the child had been fathered by someone else.

Yet if he accepted this as truth, other things he didn't want to accept became truths, as well. The words from Enrique's letter began burning a hellish path through his brain…

I remember your visit to me when you were eighteen, the scorn in your eyes for the way I'd lived my life, taking my pleasure from beautiful women at no cost to myself. Do you honestly believe you haven't pursued the very same path since then, tasting as many as you can, just because you can?

You're following my footsteps…

No, I'm different to you, Nick had thought. I'd never be so irresponsible about sowing wild oats…

But he'd done precisely what his father had done.

And he'd done it to Tess.

Of all people.

Leaving her pregnant with a child he'd known nothing about.

A son…born two months ago.

A *bastard* son.

'Miss Steele, your limousine is here.'

The announcement from the bellboy broke through Nick's fierce and tumultuous introspection. 'No!' snapped off his tongue, his free hand lifting and slamming down onto the table to reinforce his command. 'Send it away. We're not going to a movie premiere.'

'Sir!' Consternation on the guy's face. 'There's been an accident with your glass? Do you need medical attention for that cut?'

Cut? Nick's gaze jerked down to the table, taking in the spilled drink, the broken glass, the stem of which was sticking out of his grasp and stained with bleeding from the fleshy part of his hand between thumb and index finger.

'I think if you'd just fetch some tissues to form a compress?' Tess quietly suggested.

Nick glanced up to see she was staring at the wound, too.

The bellboy hesitated. 'If Mr Ramirez was served with a flawed glass…'

'It's nothing,' Nick quickly declared, not wanting a fuss. 'I'll use my handkerchief.' He whipped the dressy white triangle out of his breast pocket, set down the bit of glass he'd still been holding and wrapped up the evidence of what had obviously been a moment of madness on his part. 'Sorry about the mess,' he muttered.

'It's no trouble, sir. I'll get it cleaned up for you. About the limousine, Miss Steele...'

'Tess...' Nick growled warningly, his eyes zapping hers with a bolt of ferocious determination.

She sucked in a quick breath and conceded the change of plan. 'I won't be needing it, after all. Please let the chauffeur know I've cancelled.'

The bellboy left to do her bidding and almost simultaneously a waiter arrived to clean up *the accident*.

'You should check that the cut is minor, Nick,' Tess advised, her gaze skating away from his to fix on the handkerchief, now bound around the injury.

She was nervous, he realised, frightened of dealing with a man who was so out of control he broke glasses and didn't even know it. She was sitting back on the booth seat, hands on her lap, keeping still, trying to look cool, calm and collected, but the scarlet staining her cheekbones was evidence enough of a highly heated inner agitation—a cauldron of worries boiling behind her smooth brow.

Nick checked the wound to appease any more concern. 'Needs a Band-Aid. Nothing more,' he said dismissively, then sat back himself while the clean-up waiter did his job. Adrenaline was pumping aggression through his entire body. The hands in his lap were clenched ready to fight, wanting to fight. But reason kept telling him it was Enrique he wanted to fight, not Tess.

Tess was his solution, not his problem.

He had to deal fairly with her, kindly with her, win her compliance to what he needed, and above all, he needed to prove his bed-hopping Brazilian father was wrong about him. Deeply, essentially wrong!

'Another drink, sir?'

'No. Thank you.'

This was a time to be stone-cold sober, to have all his wits about him, channelling them into treading gently, because he had no legal rights here. Tess had his child. Tess had the Steele fortune behind her to fight any claim he might make on their son should he cross what she decided was a reasonable line. The power was all hers right now.

He had to get her to marry him.

That was absolutely paramount.

It wasn't about getting to his brothers any more.

It was about getting it right for *his own son*!

The clean-up waiter left.

'So...' Nick opened up as calmly as he could. '...you met me tonight to tell me this, Tess?'

She shook her head. 'More to test the waters, find out why you suddenly wanted to meet me. It made me wonder if you had somehow discovered...' A heavy sigh acknowledged her mistake in blabbing what could still have been kept hidden.

Nick could not soften the razor edge of his voice as he cut to the core of the situation. 'Why didn't you tell me when you first found out you were going to have my child, Tess?'

The question lay between them, loaded with currents of accusation and criticism. He saw Tess bristling, calming herself, her vivid blue eyes going hot and cold. It was impossible for him to retract the question, impossible for her to evade answering it.

'I didn't want to tell you,' she finally stated—flat, unequivocal, bluntly honest.

'Why not?' he bored in again.

She shrugged, obviously reluctant to give him any further reply. Her lashes lowered to half-mast. She lifted her hands from her lap and wrapped them around her drink, probably feeling the need for a slug of brandy.

Nick frowned over her possible motives as she raised the glass to her lips. 'Did you think I'd deny the baby could be mine?'

She sipped, set the glass down, concentrated on tipping the cinnamon pattern on top of the creamy drink from side to side. 'You were using condoms that night,' she reminded him.

'They're not one hundred percent safe, Tess, and in actual fact, one broke. That's why I asked if you were on the pill.'

Her lashes lifted, her eyes shooting a blue blaze of self-derision at him. 'I lied.'

'You lied?'

'Yes. I didn't know you were worried about a condom breaking. If you'd told me I could have taken a morning-after pill.'

'But why lie about it?'

'Because I didn't want you to know I hadn't been with anyone for so long that taking a contraceptive pill was irrelevant to my life,' she threw at him with an air of exasperation. 'You'd already cast me as an ice maiden, which I wasn't. It just seemed more...*normal*...if I said I was on the pill.' She rolled her eyes mockingly. 'I'm sure every other woman you've been with has taken care of such things. I just wasn't prepared for you. Okay?'

'And that's why you didn't want to tell me we'd made a baby?' he pressed.

Her chin came up belligerently this time, eyes flashing daggers that had clearly wounded her. 'It was a one night stand for you, remember? You didn't want any *consequences* flowing from it.'

'I just didn't want sex messing up our business relationship,' he hastily excused, hearing the passion of deeply hurt feelings building in her voice, not wanting to contribute more to them, yet unable not to press his point. 'Having a baby is something else, Tess.'

Emotion exploded from her. 'Yes, having a baby is the most essential part of being a woman and you rejected me as a woman, Nick. You rejected that part of me that made our baby, so why would I share him with you?'

Why, indeed?

Rejection hurt. He knew how badly it hurt. He hadn't realised Tess had felt that way over what he'd tried to write off as a brilliant sexual experience—one worth having by both of them.

'By the time I discovered I was pregnant...' she plunged on, her volatile tone gathering an acid note, '...you'd already plunged into an affair with another woman—an affair that went on for months—beyond the time when I dropped out of your life on the business level.'

The picture was very clear to him now. Shamingly clear. He'd run from getting into a far too heavy involvement with Tess and sought a distraction from the lure of it, caring only about what he felt, what he wanted. He'd been every bit as self-centred as his mother, choosing to be a kingpin in the battle of the sexes, not a smitten courtier.

King Rat.

That's how Tess must have seen him.

'I'm sorry.' The apology spilled off his tongue, sincerely felt yet sounding too facile even to his ears.

What else could he say?

He gestured an appeal for forgiveness, realising that he'd put her in an impossible position. Pride alone would have dictated that no intimate bond be established with him. But for the letter from Brazil and his decision to use a marriage with Tess to get to his half-brothers, his son would have been brought up without knowing a father. Which proved Enrique more right than Nick cared to acknowledge, yet acknowledge it he must.

'I'm sorry,' he repeated, even more anguished by having done so much wrong to Tess whom he truly liked and wanted to keep in his life.

The boiling anger in her eyes cooled to a simmering scepticism, making Nick acutely aware that he'd given her no grounds for believing there was any real caring behind his apology. Words were not about to convince her otherwise. Instinctively he reached across the table and took her left hand in his, intent on reforging a physical link with her. The strong sexual connection between them had created this situation. Nick automatically employed that power now to move past the mental barriers Tess held against him.

'If I'd been you, I wouldn't have told me, either,' he confessed, offering a rueful smile in the hope of lessening the tension between them. With a gentle pressure on her soft palm, he fervently added, 'I'm glad you've told me now, Tess.'

Was he?

Her gaze dropped to the hand holding hers, feeling the tingling heat transmitted by his fingers, struggling to keep her mind above the wash of sexual desire that Nick Ramirez was so adept at setting in motion. She had to concentrate on the critical issues that had been raised between them, not let her thoughts get fuzzy with distracting feelings.

Nick had been proposing marriage for the purpose of having a child. It had clearly come as a huge shock to learn he already had one but he seemed to be accepting his fatherhood without any of the aggressive protest Tess had anticipated. He was even granting she had just cause for keeping it from him.

All in all, it was an incredibly *positive* reaction from him and she found it highly confusing since it contradicted what she knew of his attitude to relationships in general. Yet it did tie in with his stated reason for proposing marriage—wanting a child with her—and the seductively subtle pressure on her left hand suggested he was still pursuing that end.

'Where is he—the baby—our son?' he asked, his voice gruff as though furred with emotion he couldn't control.

Did having a child affect him so deeply? Or was this some act to push through an agenda he was determined on carrying out by using whatever means came to hand?

'In your suite here?' he prompted when she didn't reply.

'No.' Still wary of letting Nick too close when she didn't understand where he was coming from, Tess kept her tone carefully matter-of-fact as she explained, 'I left him at home in the care of his nurse.'

'Nurse?' Alarm flashed at her.

'A Karitane nurse who specialises in helping new mothers with new babies,' she quickly explained, her mouth twitching into an ironic smile. 'I needed her more than Zack did. He's perfectly healthy, Nick.'

Relief.

Natural enough, Tess told herself. Everyone wanted a healthy child. Though she couldn't help wondering how well fatherhood would have worn with Nick if there had been something wrong with Zack. He was used to having his life running as he dictated it. What didn't suit him was very quickly jettisoned.

'Zack. You called him Zack. Is that short for Zachary?' he asked.

'No. It's just Zack.' Her chin lifted in defiance of any opinion he might hold on her choice of name for their son. 'I liked it.'

'Zack Ramirez,' he said testily. 'Not bad. Shouldn't invite any taunting variations at school. It's a name a boy can live with easily enough.'

His arrogant assumption goaded Tess into coolly correcting him. 'It's Zack Steele, not Ramirez.'

Instantly a blast of dark, dangerous energy surged into a heart-jolting challenge. 'I'm his father, Tess.'

'You'll have to convince me that fatherhood suits you, Nick,' she challenged right back, though she was rattled by his intensity.

'Then let's get started. I'll drive you home and you can introduce me to our son.'

'You want to meet him tonight?'

'Is there any reason why I shouldn't?'

She wasn't ready for it.

This wasn't what she had envisaged coming out of tonight's encounter with Nick Ramirez. Not only was he acting totally out of character but he was now set on invading her private life, having been given an in-arguable reason for doing so.

Maybe it was simply curiosity about his child driving this move—curiosity that might be quickly satisfied. It was probably best to agree to a visit right now and watch Nick in action with their baby son. If he truly did want to embrace fatherhood, well…seeing was believing, she told herself. The big problem she had with Nick's credibility this evening certainly needed some sorting out.

'Tess…' he urged, impatient with her apparent indecisiveness. His eyes were snapping with the need for quick, aggressive action. They weren't simmering with sexual promise. It was painfully evident that she wasn't really a part of what was going on inside Nick Ramirez at this moment. It was his child who'd grabbed him, wholly and solely.

'Okay. Zack will most likely be asleep and I'd prefer him not to be disturbed, but if viewing him will satisfy you…'

'Whatever's best for him,' came the swift agreement.

Nick was out of the booth and on his feet, drawing Tess from her seat without any regard for the fact that her glass was not yet empty and her chocolate cake was largely uneaten. Given his intense eagerness to see their son, any protest on a point of polite consideration seemed overwhelmingly petty. He tucked her arm around his, and Tess found herself swept along by a powerful force-field of irresistible purpose.

As always, her body was acutely conscious of his, shaming her with its wilfully wayward sexual responses when she knew sex was the last thing on Nick's mind. It might have been a weapon in his battle to win his own way earlier tonight but it was now well and truly sheathed, his mind side-tracked by Zack, his will-power trained on getting to his son.

They started down the staircase to the foyer. Most of the people below looked up at them—the women focusing on Nick, the men on her. No doubt about it—the dress she was wearing was designed to get a rise out of any male. She'd wanted to at least match— no, surpass—Nick's other women in the glamour stakes, proving she could be *hot*, too. And he had reacted. She'd succeeded in being a sex object. Except it wasn't what she really wanted, and not what he wanted, either. So it had all been for nothing…this dress…

For whatever reason, Nick had decided he wanted a child and he'd chosen her to partner him in procreation—a pragmatic choice as she was conveniently free of gold-digging ambitions, young enough to be reasonably assured of problem-free reproduction, and *comfortably* compatible in her understanding of how *his* life worked. The huge irony was—if he'd made this decision a year ago, dumped this proposition in her lap a year ago, she would have been wildly happy about it, not feeling so horribly screwed up inside.

It was eleven months too late.

Eleven months of soul devastation and heartache.

Nick had stormed her defences, taken the ultimate gift of herself, demonstrated beyond any shadow of a doubt that it had no real value to him, and she'd hated him for it—hated him because she'd loved him and he hadn't cared enough to even recognise what she'd been giving him.

At least the eleven months had left her with no illusions about what she could expect from a marriage with him. Nick would probably give her respect and courtesy, as he'd done throughout their professional relationship, plus the dubious pleasure of his company on a daily basis. He'd make the sex good for her. After all, he was an expert at it. But Tess knew she could never attach real caring—love—to his love-making.

It wasn't there.

She'd fooled herself about that once.

Never again.

Yet as long as she understood how it was with Nick and didn't expect it to change...perhaps it might not be such a bad idea to marry him. It could have benefits, especially for Zack.

Their son would have his father married to his mother—both parents together—and that was good. Zack wouldn't care how it had come about. He wouldn't know anything else, remember anything else but having them both there for him. As it should be.

As long as Nick *did* turn into the kind of father who'd be good for him.

Was he capable of selfless loving?

Tess doubted a woman would ever draw it from him, but an innocent child might—a child whose life had not yet been stamped with life's harsher lessons—a child he could shield from them. Was this what had triggered Nick's sudden drive towards fatherhood—the yen to shape a different world for a child of his own?

They'd reached the concierge's desk and Nick was ordering his car to be brought up from the parking area to the hotel entrance. Tess thought of the suite she'd booked for the night, knowing she wouldn't return to it. The butler appointed to the suite could pack her things and send them home to her tomorrow. It was just baggage—unimportant possessions, nothing that would make one whit of difference to the outcome of her life.

There was only one possession of great importance tonight.

Zack.

And how Nick responded to him.

If he couldn't feel a bond with their child, a marriage between the two of them would have no foundation worth considering. Forget sexual attraction. Forget the fantasy of loving each other for the rest of their lives. Forget the dreams of the black prince turning into her shining white knight, guarding her happiness against any encroaching shadows. Any future they might have together hinged on how much fatherhood truly meant to Nick.

That was it—plain and simple—and Tess planted that truth in the forefront of her mind, knowing she had to hang onto some common sense or she could end up being badly hurt by wanting too much from Nick Ramirez. A father for Zack—that was what this was about. His real father. And Nick Ramirez had better prove himself worthy of that title!

'Here it is,' he murmured, obviously referring to the silver Lamborghini being driven up to where they stood waiting.

Tess couldn't help tensing. Fast car…fast man… fast life…she had to be mad to even think for one moment that a family future with Nick Ramirez was even remotely possible. And she was letting him invade her life, her home, her heart…

She didn't realise her fingers had curled into claws, digging into Nick's arm. He covered her clenching hand with his, warming it with a soothing caress as he used his soft velvet voice to reduce the sudden rush of fear.

'I promise you it will be all right, Tess.' A thread of ruthless determination crept into his tone. 'I'll make it right.'

She took a deep breath. It was impossible to turn back, anyway. Nick was not about to forget he had a child. She lifted her gaze to meet and challenge the green eyes their son had inherited from his father. 'Zack looks like you but I don't want him to turn out like you, Nick. I hope you're prepared to leave a lot behind before you walk into his life tonight.'

His jawline tightened, making the intriguing little cleft in his chin more prominent, giving rise to the teasing question of how much a divided man he was between the surface Nick and the deep-down Nick. A muscle in his cheek pulsed as though it couldn't hold steady against a wave of inner pain—pain that sapped the brilliance from his eyes, leaving them flat and more unfathomable than ever.

He sighed, forcibly relaxing himself, then offered a wry little smile and said, 'Brave new world...here we come.'

The hotel parking attendant had opened the passenger door of the Lamborghini. Nick put Tess into his car, settled himself in the driver's seat, and took control of transporting them both to the central holding point of their brave new world—a nine-week-old baby who was probably fast asleep, blissfully unaware of becoming the peg on which his parents were about to hang a very different future to anything either of them had envisaged.

CHAPTER SIX

NICK barely restrained himself from flouting the speed limit. The enticing power of his Lamborghini screamed at him to put his foot down and burn up the kilometres to Tess's residence at Randwick. His son was waiting there.

But speeding didn't belong to this *brave new world* of fatherhood. Neither did a Lamborghini. The days of swinging bachelorhood were over. Tess was right. He'd better get his mind geared to leaving a lot of stuff behind.

Zack looks like you but I don't want him to be like you.

The hell of that biting statement was it echoed precisely Nick's position with his own father. He looked like Enrique but he didn't want to be like him.

Now was the time for change, for proving to himself—and Tess—that he could be a good family man, a good husband, too. She didn't believe it but she'd opened the door to him tonight—the door into a life he could share with her and their son—and Nick knew he had to keep his foot in that opening or he'd lose not only Enrique's challenge to him, but his own sense of worth as a person.

Tess had shut him out of any personal sharing all during her pregnancy, the birth, the first months of Zack's infancy. He didn't even know... 'Was he born in LA?' he shot at the mother of his child.

He heard her suck in a quick breath. He gripped the

70

driving wheel with knuckle-white intensity, reminding himself not to resent any of the decisions Tess had made, to keep the tone of any questions within a zone of warm interest and approval.

'No. He was born here in Sydney. At a private hospital in Mona Vale.' She sighed. 'I didn't go to LA, Nick. My mother doesn't need me for anything. I am truly superfluous to Livvy's life. I was superfluous to yours, too. So I used the LA location to put enough distance between us to be…out of sight, out of mind.'

He hated that self-effacing statement. He could hear the hurt of rejection behind it—the rejection he had unwittingly hit her with. 'You've owned a piece of my mind ever since we met, Tess,' he strongly asserted. 'And the longer we've known each other, the more space you've claimed there.'

He felt the sharp dart of her eyes, sensed the turmoil of vulnerability driving the silent query—whether he could be believed or not.

'I did not enjoy dealing with your PA these past six months,' he ran on, determined on correcting her view of him. 'I missed you, Tess. I missed your personal take on what I was doing. I missed the zing I always get in your company. I missed…'

'The zing?'

He flashed her a quick grin. 'The sexual battle that laced every word we spoke to each other.'

'We talked business,' she hotly argued, looking apalled at his interpretation of their meetings.

'Oh, come on,' he scoffed. 'We were always screwing with each other's heads. It was the sex we had while not having sex—thrust, parry, attacking every which way, going for whatever hit we could get, the exhilaration of matching and marking each other…'

Her hands lifted from her lap in agitation, gesturing a protest. 'It was a platonic relationship...'

'No such thing between a woman and a man when the chemistry is crackling.'

Her voice gathered more heat as she recalled, 'It was what *you* insisted we had after...'

'After we drove it too far and made it unmanageable between us?'

'Unmanageable?'

'It wasn't going to be fun any more, was it, Tess? Not after that night. It went too far too fast and felt too damned serious.'

'Does sex *have* to be fun to you?' she flung at him irritably.

'Fun doesn't end up clawing at you,' he argued. 'It's froth and bubble. The high, without any of the lows. The minute sex gets serious, all the negative stuff starts happening...possessiveness, jealousy, slavish obsession, manic arguments. People make fools of themselves, victims of their own raging hormones. I didn't think that was a good place for us to progress to.'

'Because the sex felt...too serious?'

He could hear her thinking her way around what he was saying, beginning to feel less sexually diminished by his retreat from physical intimacy with her.

'I valued what we had too much to risk it on passion running wild, getting out of control in a big way,' he pressed on. 'I wanted to keep you in my life without the aggravation of feeling owned by you.'

A hysterical little laugh gurgled from her throat. 'Better get used to the sense of being *owned*, Nick...if you have the heart of a father.'

Another shafting challenge.

The sexual stand-off was still in place, as far as Tess was concerned. Tonight was not about fun and games between a man and a woman. Tonight was about how he responded to their son.

And the mind-crawling truth was...he was being judged.

The sense of King Rat's integrity being on the chopping block was strong from the moment he entered the old colonial-styled mansion Tess used as both her business premises and home.

The nurse who greeted them at the front door was instantly told, 'This is Nick Ramirez, Zack's father.'

The father who had been conspicuous by his absence since the birth of his son.

That knowledge was certainly in the nurse's measuring eyes as she escorted them to the nursery upstairs, answering Tess's questions about Zack's evening—no problems—hadn't woken for his night feed yet. She left them at the nursery door, retreating from what had to be huge private business. The judgement axe was sharpening up in Tess's eyes as she ushered him into a room lit by a soft night lamp and dominated by a white cane bassinette which stood under a host of mobile objects strung from the ceiling.

Nick's entire body was gripped with electric tension as he faced the piece of furniture holding the child he'd made with Tess. Suddenly he was racked with uncertainty over whether he was capable of passing the fatherhood test. Was he prepared to cede power over his life to another human being...to be *owned*?

He forced his feet forward, fiercely telling himself it was too late to be carrying out any self-examination. Besides, there was no decision to be made here. The baby in the bassinette was his flesh and blood, irrevocably linked to him. They owned each other—had owned each other from the moment Zack had been conceived, and would own each other for as long as life went on. It was the quality of the ownership that was on the line.

The turbulence churning through Nick miraculously calmed once he'd reached the bassinette and his gaze finally rested on the living breathing object of all his angst.

'So tiny…' The incredulous comment whispered from his lips on a wave of awe.

'Zack is actually big for his age,' Tess dryly informed him.

Big?

Nick shook his head.

This baby was shockingly tiny and all swaddled up like a miniature Egyptian mummy in a blue and white checked cloth. Only his face was on show—a fine little face with properly proportioned features, nothing too big or too small, ears nestled tightly to the side of his head—important for a boy.

He had lots of black hair in corkscrew ringlets which could be embarrassing—very girly—as were the crescents of long, thick eyelashes fanned out across his cheeks, but attitude was the key to stopping any teasing on that score. Nick figured he could teach his son attitude. A *pretty boy* tag wouldn't last long.

The slight dimple in the centre of his chin was like a magnet, drawing Nick's finger into touching the genetic blueprint that belonged to both of them. Unbelievably soft skin. Nick couldn't resist feeling more of it, finger-feathering the delicately drawn jawline from ear to ear, smiling as his son emitted a snuffling little sigh. Nick sent him a mental message—*Hi, Zack. This is your father standing by.*

It was like a trigger for action. The swathed bundle started squirming, feet kicking out for freedom, hands punching at the constricting cloth. The finely arched baby brows dipped into a surprisingly adult frown and the rosebud mouth gulped for air a couple of times, then poured forth a full-blooded scream, proving his lungs were working at top capacity.

It startled Nick into turning to Tess in alarm. 'I didn't hurt him.'

She shook her head, smiling as she explained, 'It's just Zack's stomach clock going off. Time for his night feed. Would you like to pick him up and soothe him while I heat up his bottle?'

'Pick him up,' Nick muttered, his hands diving under the miniature bundle, eager to gather it up for a much closer and more personal encounter. It moved. It made itself heard in no uncertain terms. It was not some passive doll-like creature. This was his son!

'Mind you support his head, Nick,' Tess quickly instructed. 'He's not strong enough yet to hold it up on his own.'

'Got it!'

The loud bawling stopped the minute the baby was airborne. In a very swift maneouvre Nick had him tucked safely against his chest, head resting in the crook of his arm. If rocking was required, action stations had been reached, but Zack had apparently decided he didn't need soothing, or the distraction of being handled by a stranger had put a hold on further complaint. He was well and truly awake now and weighing Nick up with highly alert eyes—green eyes!

Father? they seemed to be asking. *What the devil is a father and do I want him standing by?*

'Yes, you do,' Nick heard himself crooning. 'You can trust me on that, Zack.'

'What?' Tess queried, distracted from getting a bottle of milk out of a mini-fridge and putting it in a microwave oven.

Her voice ended the moment of peace. Zack was far more familiar with his mother and promptly yelled for her. Trust clearly had to be earned and as far as their son was concerned, Nick hadn't been hanging around long enough to earn it.

'You've had a head start on me at soothing, Tess,' he excused when rocking had no calming effect and she came over to take Zack from him.

'I'll change his nappy while the milk is warming up,' she said briskly, carrying him off to a highly functional trolley loaded with a comprehensive range of baby toiletries.

Nick followed on her heels, wanting to see his son unwrapped from the cloth cocoon. Besides which, he needed to conquer the mystery of nappy-changing so he couldn't be accused of being useless on the baby front. The urge to be a hands-on father who automatically commanded Zack's trust was powering through him. *Standing by* was not enough. Bonding obviously came from real involvement in his life. Nick had some fast catching up to do to match Tess in the parental stakes.

Once laid on the flat trolley surface, Zack fought free of the constricting cloth with very little help from Tess—arms and legs going like pistons, determination to be rid of this imprisonment clearly written on his little face. Tess had quite a job undoing the press-studs on the blue body-suit he wore, her hands darting around all the kicking and squirming. However, he did lie still while she whipped off his nappy—an easy matter of opening two contact tabs.

Before Nick could get a good look of his son's *male* equipment, Tess had placed a small towel over it.

'What's with the modesty?' he protested. 'Seems to me Zack likes to get naked.'

'Yes. And the first thing he does on getting naked is let fly with a fountain of pee. We're right in his firing range but if you want to risk it...'

Even as she spoke, the towel was developing a wet patch and Nick found himself grinning at the look of blissful pleasure on Zack's face. 'Mother knows best,' he told his son and didn't care that he sounded fatuous. Two sets of green eyes were telegraphing a very mutual understanding of male instinct at each other.

'You can check him out now,' Tess tersely invited as she removed the absorbent towel and dropped it in a bucket. 'I'm not qualified to comment on the size of a baby boy's private parts, but the paediatrician who delivered him observed that Zack was built like a bull, and from this admiring approval I assume that our son needn't be concerned about looking suitably virile.'

A bull certainly seemed an exaggeration, but Nick was pleased to see this special area was absolutely free of problems. 'Nothing worse for a guy than feeling inadequate about his masculinity,' he explained, glad of the paediatrician's opinion. *Everything* was so *tiny*!

Tess threw him a derisive look as she covered Zack up with a fresh nappy. 'Hardly a feeling you'd be familiar with.'

'It's not just men who care about size, Tess,' he sliced back at her.

'I'm sure all the women you've had were very satisfied, Nick. I just don't want Zack to think he has to sample every female passing by because he's well endowed.'

'I do not and never have sampled every woman passing by,' Nick protested. 'I hope you're not going to load Zack up with a neurotic mess of unnatural inhibitions.'

She'd done up the press-studs, completing Zack's dressing, and with the confidence of plenty of practice she scooped him up and planted him against her shoulder. 'Guess you might have to stick around and make sure I don't,' she slung at him, scarlet flags in her cheeks again as she headed back to the microwave oven for the bottle of milk.

Another challenge.

Plus the major point that she was in the box seat...the one in control over their son's life. Nick saw very clearly that it wasn't just a matter of getting married but *staying* married if he was to have serious input on all the decisions that would shape Zack's future. And Tess was in the box seat there, as well. She didn't have to marry him and she'd already proven he was expendable. He had to change her thinking on that, make himself valuable to her.

She settled onto a rocking chair with Zack already attached to the teat of the bottle. Anger at her implied criticism of his life choices spilled into the terse comment. 'I'm surprised you're not breast-feeding. Isn't mother's milk best for babies?'

'I couldn't breast-feed. There were...' She grimaced. '...complications.'

He frowned. Tess had great breasts. He couldn't believe they had failed their prime function. Nick knew his own mother scorned the practice of breast-feeding—*peasant women who want to be cows*—rattling on about the old aristocracy having had it right with employing wet-nurses for their children. Was Tess lying, making excuses for the vanity of not wanting sagging breasts in future?

'What complications?' he asked.

'You don't really want to know the gory details, Nick,' she said dismissively.

Alarm streaked through him as her comment triggered a flurry of fears. 'I most certainly do.'

She winced at his persistence. 'Zack was born perfectly healthy.'

His mind zapped to the other side of the equation. 'But you weren't so healthy, Tess?'

She sighed. 'He was just a big baby. I wanted a natural birth but he seemed to get stuck in the birth canal and I didn't want him to be pulled out by instruments so I elected to have a Caesarean operation instead.'

Sounded like one hell of a birth process to Nick.

'Anyhow, Zack came out of it fine, but I ended up with an infection from the operation and had to be given antibiotics...'

'Making you too sick to breast-feed.'

'For a while I was too sick to do anything for Zack.'

Hence the private nurse, specialising in baby-care. All the more understandable now, yet Tess could surely have done with personal support throughout these painful difficulties. 'I should have been there. You should not have gone through this on your own.'

'I wasn't on my own.'

'No doubt the medical staff at your private hospital was adequate but...'

'Dad sat with me.'

'No…' The word burst from an instant welling of violent protest. Before Nick could even begin to monitor what he was saying or why, his mind spewed out a furious bank of resentment. 'You put *your* father in *my* place? You let *my* child be born a bastard like me and had Brian Steele witness it all?'

He could not contain the outrage, his hands flying out in emphatic fury. 'My God, Tess! However you judge the way I've lived my life, to shame me like that, to choose the man who showed me his door because I wasn't his flesh-and-blood son, to choose him to sit by you when it was *my son* being born…*my son*…'

'He's my father,' she countered fiercely. 'And the only person I've ever been able to count on to give me support when I needed it.'

'You didn't ask me, dammit! You didn't tell me! You didn't give me the chance to be there for you! To be there for both of you!'

Their raised voices broke Zack's concentration on the contents of his bottle. He abandoned the teat to yell his displeasure in the bad vibrations swirling around him.

Tess lifted him to her shoulder again to rub his back soothingly, her eyes snapping an urgent plea at Nick. 'Can we leave this until I put him down to sleep again?'

Nick's entire body clenched as he forced it to contain the offence he felt. His mind seethed with the rejection she had slapped on him, never mind the rejection she'd suffered at his hands. It took every ounce of control he had to give her a grim-faced nod and turn away from the sight of her *owning* his child as though he didn't count for anything in their lives.

He was going to count all right!

He was going to count as Tess's partner in raising their son and he was going to count as Zack's father and that was going to start happening tonight!

CHAPTER SEVEN

TESS could not calm her fluttering heart. She felt as though she was in a cage with a wild animal prowling around—a dangerous animal holding fire until it was time to attack without causing collateral damage. As long as Zack was in her arms she was safe, but once he was put back in the bassinette for the night, Nick was set to erupt again, giving vent to the violent feelings he'd obviously been suppressing since he'd broken the glass at the hotel.

This passionately raging Nick bore no resemblance to the ultra-smooth sophisticated man she'd known— the charming user who cynically knew the value of everything, was amused by how those values worked, and let very little really touch him.

There was nothing at all civilised about the depth of caring that had just exploded from him. He certainly found no *fun* in this situation. It was clawing at him every which way, and the inescapable fact that she was Brian Steele's daughter was far from irrelevant.

The past was not in the past. Not tonight. Birth…marriage…they were cycles of life, spiralling back into previous events that invariably influenced the future, touching off connections that never went away even though they might be shunned. It was impossible to close those connections out and pretend they didn't exist, didn't carry any weight. Nick's past had just come screaming alive, and while Tess knew where it was coming from, it didn't make it any easier to face.

Zack snoozed off before completely emptying the bottle of milk, burping contentedly against her shoulder as she carried him over to the change table to wrap him up snugly again. She was acutely conscious of Nick standing by, watching her every move, his gaze trained exclusively on his son until Zack was laid in the bassinette, looking at peace with his small innocent world. No emotional scars for him yet. Tess hoped he would never have any bad baggage to carry.

Her skin literally prickled with nervous tension as she led Nick out of the nursery quarters and across the wide central corridor of the upper floor to her own private apartment. 'There are electronic monitors so that both I and the nurse can hear if Zack is disturbed, no matter where we are,' she explained as she closed the door, trying to maintain a matter-of-fact air.

'I'm sure you've been meticulous in setting up a safe environment.'

The clipped reply put an even tighter band around her chest. Nick's resentment at having been left out of everything was coming through loud and clear. She watched him taking in her personal living area, moving to open the door to her bedroom suite, casing that space, as well.

'We'd better start looking for a family home, Tess. This won't do for both of us with Zack, any more than my apartment at Woolloomooloo will,' he said, his green eyes shooting unassailable determination at her.

Tess felt her knees go weak. Apparently Nick was now intent on bulldozing her into marriage, mentally overriding objections from her before she'd even made them. He'd spoken fiercely of *his* rights, but he was just as blind to the concerns underlining her decisions as she'd been to his.

'Dad didn't know you were my baby's father, Nick,' she blurted out. 'I didn't tell him. I still haven't. He was by my side at the hospital because I wanted someone to watch over me in case…in case anything went wrong.'

Nick's chest visibly expanded. Tess didn't know if he was taking in much needed air or containing a volatile response. A frantic urge to set the record completely straight sent words tumbling out of her mouth, wanting to reach him before terrible mistakes were made.

'I wasn't going to tell you, either. I met you tonight because Dad made me see it would eventually be very wrong to keep hiding your identity from Zack. He recalled that your mother did that to you, Nick, keeping you in the dark as to who your real father was, and how much it had hurt you. He said Zack had the right to know. But for this very strongly stated advice, I might have denied you any knowledge of your son.'

'No. I would have come after you, Tess.' He moved back towards her, his powerful body emanating a ruthless air of confidence, his eyes burning with purpose. 'I was already in the process of coming after you.'

Her breath caught in her throat, rendering her speechless as his hands slid around her waist, drawing her lower body into contact with his. Her own hands, having been lifted in appeal for his understanding, landed automatically on his chest and were instantly tempted into sliding higher to his shoulders as her face tilted up to read the expression on his.

'And nothing would have stopped me,' he asserted with a wry twist of his mouth. One arm clamped her very securely to him as he raised the other and grazed soft fingertips down her cheek, his eyes engaging hers very intently in apologetic appeal. 'I'm sorry we arrived at this place in this way, Tess, but we're here, and *you* are the woman I want to be here with.'

Was she?

He had proposed marriage before he knew about Zack, so she was definitely the wife of his choice against all other comers. And since there'd been such a formidable list of stunningly beautiful and remarkably talented women in his life, she should probably feel flattered, even elated that he had chosen her, not torn by fears of being fooled and used.

As though he could see the emotional chaos consuming her, he thickly murmured, 'Right now I'm hauling you in from the months that have separated us...' His head was bending, his mouth coming closer and closer to hers, breathing words onto her lips. '...from the misunderstanding that drove you away from me. I didn't stop wanting you, Tess...'

He kissed her. He kissed her in a way that stole her heart all over again—a kiss that started with tender reassurance, slid into seductive persuasion, incited erotic excitement, then burst into a passionate claim on all she was. There was no resistance in Tess to the marauding power of his desire. She wanted to feel it, wanted to lose herself in it, wanted to wallow in the sense that Nick Ramirez was hers—hers to have and to hold until...

No, she wouldn't think beyond this moment.

Everything within her was pulsing with pleasure in the wild passion he emitted and evoked, so why not just let herself indulge in the dream of his loving her for as long he brought her to this brilliant pitch of vibrant life?

Yes was dancing through her mind.

Yes was humming through her bloodstream.

She didn't want to listen to anything else.

His mouth broke from hers to gulp in air. He was holding her so tightly now, her breasts lifted with his chest as he refilled his lungs. It was like riding the crest of a wave, exhilarating, an intimate connection with natural forces that swept her along without any decision-making being required.

His lips trailed hot little kisses across her cheek to her ear. The words he whispered were like heady wine, sweetly intoxicating. 'One taste of you and I'm drowning again, Tess. If I were an old-time sailor on a journey, I'd never get past your siren song to go anywhere.'

But he had gone elsewhere.

To another woman.

And if he did that again…

A sudden savage surge of primitive possessiveness had her reaching up, grabbing his head, pulling it back, her eyes targeting his with a blazing warning. 'You take the step of marrying me, you stay with me, Nick. If you stray…don't even try to come back. The door will be closed to you and it will stay closed.'

'The owning,' he drawled, his mouth twitching with mocking amusement, his eyes dancing with devilment. 'Understood, Tess, but in all fairness I get to own you, too.' His fingers raked through her hair. 'I fancy seeing this crowning glory of yours spread in fiery abandonment across black satin pillows. *My* pillows. Whenever I want it there.'

He meant very visibly naked, which instantly stirred

up all Tess's physical insecurities. He'd been naked with a whole tribe of gym-toned, perfectly body-sculpted women. Her mind marched to defensive stations, commanding a dampening down of ardour.

'Bad luck! I've only got chocolate-brown cotton on my bed if you're thinking of using it tonight.'

He laughed. 'That's my Tess! But no way is the image in my mind deflated,' he said with relish, then swooped and swept her right off her feet, cradling her across his chest as easily as he'd cradled Zack. 'Must try it out. Black might be a bit stark. Chocolate-brown could be a warmer contrast, especially for the pearly gleam of your skin.'

Pearly gleam...

Nick had sampled so many carefully tanned women, she'd thought he'd see her as washed-out white, but *pearly gleam* sounded attractive. Even enticing. And there really was nothing *wrong* with her body. He'd simply made her feel it wasn't up to *his mark* when he'd dumped her after only one night.

She needed him to erase the long miserable hang-over from that rejection.

She needed him to make her feel so intensely desirable, no other woman could ever lure him into being unfaithful.

This was probably stretching the dream too far but hope was taking wing and Tess had no heart for tethering it. Indeed, her heart was pumping so hard and fast, it felt like a highly fateful drum-roll, heralding in what had to be a brave new world with Nick.

He set her on her feet beside the bed, viewing it approvingly over her shoulder. The quilt was actually made of dark brown and taupe silk squares in a checked pattern. These colours were repeated in a pile of decorator cushions with some gold brocade and tassels thrown in for added richness.

'Very sensual, seductive and sumptuous,' Nick observed. 'Just like you, Tess.'

'It's cotton underneath,' she whipped back, then wished she could tear her tongue out. Why couldn't she just accept the compliment, take it as a fortunate reflection of how he saw her? What was she fighting against?

The answer flashed like a neon light across the churning mess in her mind.

The surface stuff!

She hated the surface stuff...all the glittering gorgeous women Nick had preferred to her, women like his *Miss Universe* mother, strutting through his life, the silk and satin women with all their gold accessories, gathering their status symbols, including Nick Ramirez amongst them, the Latin lover to surpass all others.

She'd been instinctively fighting it ever since she'd met Nick and couldn't stop herself even now when she had him—fool that she was, dismissing what obviously grabbed his attention.

'I know it's cotton underneath and that's like you, too—sensible, practical, longer—lasting, wash and wear, easy and comfortable to live with,' Nick rolled out as though revelling in both sides of her, his eyes teasing her insistence on flouting his flattery, seeming to enjoy her perversity.

'Oh, great! That puts me in the same class as a pair of old underpants,' tripped straight off her wayward tongue.

'No, you're in a class of your own.' He withdrew his hand from her hair and pressed a light finger to her lips, the amusement in his eyes winking out as an emerald-fire intensity flared over it. 'You don't have to keep telling me you're different to all the other women who've peopled my life. I hear it, I see it, I feel it, I taste it, I smell it. Every sense I have is constantly pointing it out to me.'

Right! So keep your mouth shut, Tess!

'The whole problem was...' he ran on '...you didn't fit into my picture. So this time around, I'm beginning with you as the centrepiece and waiting and watching for the picture to develop around you. So let me focus on you, Tess. We will inevitably get to the cotton, but don't deny the pleasure there is in the sumptuous sexuality you personify tonight.'

Wicked pleasure.

Designed to impact on him and give her the secret thrill of knowing it did. The battle of the sexes... another piece of compelling strategy. Nick knew it but it didn't matter that he knew it because there *was* pleasure in it for both of them...pleasure in the simmering sensuality in his eyes as he stroked the silky red ringlets that shimmered with artificial gold, as he caressed the sensitive nape of her neck and slowly, slowly, slid the supporting straps of her body-flaunting dress from her shoulders, holding her in spellbound anticipation for more exquisite and intimate touches.

Nick knew how to kiss.

He knew how to touch.

The memory of their one previous night together was racing along her nerves, making them tremble with excitement. She closed her eyes as his gaze fell to the soft slopes of her breasts, the pads of his fingers grazing up and down, easing aside the filmy fabric, pushing closer and closer to the peaks.

'Just as well Zack didn't ever learn what he's missing out on or he'd be screaming with frustration every time you give him a bottle,' Nick murmured, cupping the full weight of one of her breasts and using his thumb to circle the now rock-hard aureole and nipple, making her ache for the maternal experience *she* was missing. 'You were built for babies, Tess. And nothing is more sexy to a man…lovely soft, full breasts…'

He bent to kiss them, to gently suck on them, making every muscle in her body contract and quiver from the shafts of deep pleasure arcing from his mouth. His hands found the zipper at the back of her bodice, opened it, and the sheer weight of the layered and beaded skirt—no longer fastened to her waist—pulled the whole dress down into a flurry of frills around her feet. Only her mauve silk-and-lace panties saved her from being totally naked in front of him.

And he was still fully dressed!

'Look at you…' he said as he straightened up and stepped back from her, his hands lightly hooked on the curve of her hips near the elastic band of her panties, making her acutely aware of where his thumbs would move next.

'I'd rather look at you,' croaked from her hopelessly dry throat. She was burning up from the sudden rush of almost complete exposure, from her helpless response to Nick's expertise in fuelling sexual excitement.

'But you're far more exotic. And erotic,' he declared, grinning with wicked delight. 'Fantastic fire and ice with those diamond earrings dangling against your hair and the pendant nestling where it is…' His

gaze sizzled down to her cleavage. 'Not to mention...'
He tugged the panties down, his voice thickening as
her most private place was revealed. '...snow-white
thighs divided by a flaming arrow of hair.'

Her mind simply blew under the pressure of being
so nakedly on show. His words probably should have
banished the sense of his having preferred other
women, but somehow they triggered a tormenting
storm of stomach-wrenching comparisons.

'I would have thought a Brazilian wax job was more
to your taste,' she snapped.

He shook his head. 'It bares what should be a teasing mystery. You, Tess...' He swept her off her feet
and onto the bed, placing a knee between her thighs,
accelerating her pounding sense of utter vulnerability.
'...you...' he growled emphatically, his eyes sizzling
with satisfaction in the wild spill of her hair over the
rich chocolate cushions. '...are the epitome of visual
sexiness.'

True or not, Tess fiercely told herself to stop wor-
rying about it. She could concentrate on him now. He
was taking off his formal jacket, tossing it onto the
floor. The black bowtie was swiftly pulled apart, the
studs on his pristine pin-tucked shirt pushed open, cuf-
flinks removed and dropped into a trouser pocket.

Her breath literally caught in her throat as he finally
discarded the dress shirt. Photographs of beautiful men
in the raw—even seeing them in action on movie or
television screens—did not have the physical impact
of the real thing.

Nick Ramirez was perfectly muscled where a man
was supposed to be muscled and the shape of him was
all in such elegant proportion it was positively awe-
some—the leashed power in his broad shoulders, the

strong width of chest, his torso tapering with athletic precision to a flat stomach—but most stunning of all, the sudden expanse of satin-smooth skin, darkly gleaming with a kind of animal vitality that was totally mesmerising.

Even as her gaze gloated over his glorious masculinity, he was stripping off the rest of his clothes, adding to the magnetic enticement of power-packed manhood. She wanted to touch, wanted to taste, knew there couldn't be a woman on earth who wouldn't wish to have him available to her like this, wanting exactly what she wanted.

Nick was offering himself to *her* tonight.

Tess reached out and took, her hands gliding slowly, revelling in the silky heat of him, feeling it fire up the hectic and hungry desire already coursing through her blood, exciting her with the exhilarating knowledge that underneath this satin skin he was pumped up and hard with arousal.

Her mind filled with a wild wanton joy as she caressed him more intimately, provocatively, exulting in his desire for her, savagely wanting to drive it to blinding, deafening heights where he could see only her, hear only her, feel only her, know only her.

The groan from deep in his throat sounded anguished as he left the bed momentarily to rid himself of the last of his clothes. His eyes were like bolts of green lightning, zigzagging over her body, shooting electric tension into all the high spots, raising tremors in all her muscles, making her pulse race at the promise of intense stimulation to come.

He looked magnificent, smooth and dark and so sexually male, her heart quailed at the terrible soul-wrenching need to keep him to herself. The yearning to possess clutched at her stomach. Her breasts ached with it. A wild cry broke from her throat as he brought all his dynamic aggressive energy down to her, the full body contact making her arch into him and driving her arms and legs to wind shamelessly around him, demanding an instant appeasement of the fierce hunger inside her.

It came, hard and fast, a wild rocketing plunge that steamed straight through her moist heat, pounding its urgency to claim the innermost depths of her, not once, not twice, but a wild barrage of possession—a blisteringly primal coupling that drove them both to the edge of intolerable yet torturously exquisite tension.

His eyes blazed a highly dominant basic challenge at her—determined on holding control, maintaining the forceful rhythm until she broke it by shattering into climax. The dark strain on his face, the thin-lipped grimness of his mouth, the jut of his chin—all spoke of what it was costing him, but cost was no object when it came to winning for Nick. Most notably with women.

For Tess this was a soul-deep contest. She refused to be an easy lay for him. Let him wait. Let *his* limits be tested. Let his arrogant confidence in his sexual expertise take a knock for once. She revelled in the sense of teetering on the brink of orgasm, holding on as long as she could, working her inner muscles to squeeze him into surrendering to her first, fizzing around him with wickedly voluptuous provocation, gritting her teeth against the mounting waves of tumultuous sensation, hanging on because it bound him to her so intensely there was no room for thought of anything or anyone else.

He was hers.

All hers.

And with that ecstatic thought tap-dancing all over her tightly focused concentration, Tess lost the battle, her muscles rippling convulsively along the powerful length of his shaft, the out of control flutters swirling into a swamping tidal wave of pleasure that lifted her to an incredible crest of creaming bliss and spilled her into sweet heavenly contentment.

She heard him cry out and it sounded like the triumphant shout of a winner who'd completely spent himself in winning, making the victory more deeply prized, but she didn't feel beaten as she felt the erratic spasms of his release. Her nerve-endings tingled with an exultant awareness of their ultimate fusion, giving her the sense of a very exclusive sharing…a richer, deeper, mutual fulfilment than could ever be achieved with anyone else.

Tess clung to that belief as the physical intensity of their intimacy eased into a languidly comfortable nestling, Nick's arm around her shoulders, her head resting on his chest, their soft breathing attuned to a relaxed togetherness.

'I've heard it said that the secret to a successful marriage is lots of sex,' Nick murmured, the deep timbre of his voice rumbling up from his chest, resonating in her ear.

Other people might have said loving each other, Tess thought, the dreamy happiness in her heart fraying around the edges as his reality chewed on it.

Would a constant barrage of *making love* keep Nick satisfied with his commitment?

She hadn't yet consented to marry him but the temptation to give in and take what he was offering— if only for the pleasure no other man had ever given her—was very strong. She feathered her fingers over his tautly packed flesh and felt the faint quivers under his skin, knowing he was excitingly sensitised to her touch, revelling in the knowledge.

'I don't see myself as a wife who would have headaches,' she said whimsically.

As her hand drifted below his hip-bone, towards his groin, he plucked it off him and carried it to the pillow beside her head, rolling her onto her back, taking command of the situation.

'To have and to hold from this day forth,' he intoned, his eyes glittering purposeful satisfaction in his domination. 'No messing with that vow, Tess?'

'It goes both ways, Nick,' she reminded him, not conceding anything.

'Fine. As long as you're ready for it. It's a very powerful weapon—desire—and women like testing it, but don't ever stir it unless you're prepared to match what you stir. Understood?'

Power...the idea of having any sexual power over Nick hadn't entered Tess's head. It amazed her that he felt she did have it. She'd viewed her whole association with him as being entirely the other way.

'Tease...and I'll take it as an invitation,' he ran on, the glitter changing to a hard, ruthless gleam as he added, 'Try bartering with it and I'll walk.'

No bartering with sex.

Tess mentally wrote the rule in her mind although it seemed to run contrary to everything she thought Nick had stood for. Surely it was how his world worked—selling everything with sex.

'Understood, Tess?' he repeated, his eyes boring into hers so intensely, he left her in no doubt this was a prime requirement for a workable relationship between them.

'Yes,' she agreed.

He released her hand and moved his to trace her lips with feathering fingertips. 'Power is a fine balancing act,' he murmured.

He wanted it in his hands, Tess thought.

Then he bent his head and kissed her, and she didn't care if he always had sexual power over her.

As long as she remained desirable to him.

Uniquely desirable.

The one and only woman he wanted.

This might only be a dream—a foolish dream that couldn't possibly last—but Tess wanted to hang onto it as long as she could.

CHAPTER EIGHT

FROM the time Zack woke them the next morning, Nick started operating on the presumption that Tess would marry him, no question about whether it *was* actually settled between them. Watching him with their baby son—his pleasure in sharing this new life— Tess could not bring herself to disabuse him of the idea.

Let it ride for the moment, she decided.

See how long Nick's keenness for it lasted.

He did not leave until after breakfast, and only then with the declared intention of returning within an hour or two, once he'd collected the legal forms they had to fill out and have officially filed in order to get married.

Tess waved him off in his flash silver Lamborghini, wondering in a somewhat bemused fashion if he'd drive back in a sedate family sedan. The air seemed to be crackling with changes coming so fast, she was grateful for the respite from Nick's presence, needing some time and space to come to grips with a proposal she would have declared impossible yesterday.

As she turned to go inside, her gaze swept around the old white weatherboard colonial mansion she had transformed to suit herself and her business. It was perfectly sited here at Randwick; close to the inner city, close to Fox Studios, and close to the National Institute for Dramatic Art. Its semicircular driveway— previously a carriageway—provided off-street parking for clients, and the downstairs rooms housed not only her casting agency but also a top photographers' studio so that portfolios could be created under her guiding eye.

She had always liked the gracious style of the place, its wide verandahs with their ornate white iron-lace finish and the old-fashioned bullnose iron roof which was painted the same dark green as the Norfolk pines that stood in the grounds. Somehow it presented a statement of lasting quality, of class that was by no means diminished by the changing architectural styles demanded by modern society.

But Nick was right. While it would still have suited her as a single mother—the perfect set-up, in fact—being married to him and establishing a family unit would definitely mean moving.

Where to and to what?

Tess couldn't get her mind around that, either. The sense of still being in dreamworld was too strong for such down-to-earth decisions. All she knew with absolute certainty was she was not about to sell this place. It represented the life she'd made for herself—a life she trusted.

Trust was very much on her mind when Nick returned with the legal forms, intent on nailing their marriage down. Zack was having his mid-morning nap upstairs, so Tess was in her office, going over the list of new contracts her PA had organised. The moment Nick was ushered in, he was commandeering her desk, laying out the documents, handing her a pen, instructing what was needed and where, pouring out the energy that automatically swept people along with him, doing his will.

'Once I lodge these at the register office with the

relevant documents—copies of our birth certificates—
we have to wait a month,' he informed her, hitching
himself onto the front of the desk, arrogantly taking
up a position of dominant control.

A month, she thought. Was a month long enough
for testing how genuine Nick's commitment was to
both herself and Zack?

'Which means we'll be running into Christmas and
New Year,' he ran on, 'making the best function
places a difficult proposition. But I thought if we employed a top wedding planner, got the invitations out
straight away...'

'Stop!'

He glowered at her suspiciously as she put the pen
down and rolled her chair back from his overbearing
and highly distracting vicinity. 'Stop what?' he demanded.

She clutched at the common sense she'd been working on before he'd returned. 'I've had some time to
think about this, Nick.'

A thunderous tension instantly descended. 'Don't
tell me you've changed your mind.'

'I haven't once said I would marry you,' she stated
sharply, refusing to be intimidated by the pressure of
his will. 'In fact, you've given me very little time to
consider your proposal.'

'What's to consider? We have a duty of care to our
son which is best served by the two of us getting married. Given your background and my own, how can
there possibly be any argument between us over that?'

Flustered by his ruthless logic, Tess seized on her
main uncertainty. 'What about us?'

'I thought we settled *us* last night. Did we or did

we not lay down the rules for our marriage to work? *And* reach a mutual understanding over them.'

In the heat of the night, yes, but...

'What's the point of backtracking now, Tess? Just sign the papers and give it a chance.' His eyes glittered at her in hard, relentless challenge. 'Remember how it was for you as a kid—lost between Livvy's and your father's worlds. I sure as hell remember how it was for me—not wanted by anyone, shuttled aside to fend for myself. We have to make it different for Zack. For his sake, you must see our marriage as the best way.'

Give it a chance...

For Zack's sake...

Yes. Her mind seized on the cogent argument of their own wretched childhoods. It was the right thing—the only fair thing—to do for their son. To at least try a marriage with Nick.

She was probably putting her heart on the chopping block, but on the positive personal side, she wouldn't have a cold lonely bed for as long as Nick kept faith with his commitment. She might as well take the pleasure he was offering while she could.

'Okay!' she decided, rolling her chair back to the desk and proceeding to sign the forms with a sense of reckless determination. She was probably a fool, taking fool's gold, but until this marriage was proven worthless, she would give it a chance. For Zack's sake!

'But I don't want a big social wedding,' she said emphatically, putting the pen down and facing Nick with her decision.

'Why not?' His eyes narrowed in fiercely probing assessment. 'Neither of us is planning to do this again.

It's a one-off, Tess. Why not do the big splash...the whole fairy-tale wedding that all women want?'

'For one thing, it wouldn't be a fairy-tale wedding.' Her own eyes mocked that impossible concept as she pressed the inescapable truth. 'More like a three-ring circus.'

He frowned.

'Think about it, Nick,' she invited derisively, her hands gesturing the grand scale of what would inevitably occur. 'It wouldn't be a wonderful personal occasion. It would be the gossipfest of the year—my father and his three wives in attendance—your mother and my mother competing for the limelight—the bride who *is* Brian Steele's daughter and the groom who turned out to be *not* his son...'

The dark frown lifted as his mouth twitched with sardonic humour. 'Could be quite amusing to have them all dancing to our tune.'

His cynical view of their family situation completely missed the point. 'Do you imagine anyone would actually be there to wish us well?' she threw at him in exasperation, thinking of all the bitchy A-list women who'd hate her for *roping in* the man they'd targeted.

She could hear them now—

The good old pregnancy trap...

The Steele billions behind her...

Nothing to do with love, darling...

Nick shrugged. 'Humanity is as it is. We swim in that stream, Tess, and so will our son. Hiding from it won't make it go away.'

'But we don't have to play to the gallery,' she protested, her innate sense of self-protection forbidding the taking of that road.

'What alternative do you have in mind?' he shot at her, his face hardening. 'Running away?'

'Yes…no…I mean…just choosing how I'd like our wedding to be, Nick,' she pleaded, still grasping at the chance that what he promised would work out. 'I was thinking very private…'

'You can't keep our marriage a permanent secret any more than you could have kept our son a secret, and putting off facing people with the truth only makes it harder,' he argued in harsh warning, then tempered his tone to a gentler note as he added, 'There's no shame in our situation, Tess. I'll be right at your side, protecting you from…'

'No!' She pushed up from her chair in agitation at feeling pressured to perform in the public eye. 'Whose voice are you listening to, Nick?' she flared at him in fiery challenge. 'What focus do you have on our wedding day?'

'My focus is on being completely upfront, not hiding anything about us, Tess,' he drilled back at her.

Heat burned her cheeks at the implied criticism of her less open stance. 'Oh? Funny how I thought this marriage was only about you and me and Zack!' she countered. 'When did it start developing other more public agendas?'

She flung the question at him as she rounded the desk and moved away, turning her back on *his focus*. It wasn't that she couldn't brave other people's opinions and attitudes. It wasn't that she couldn't defy them. She could and would face them when she had to…but not *before* her wedding to Nick Ramirez and not *at it*!

The *surface stuff* would count for too much.

The dream would be tarnished by it.

If they were married privately just before Christmas and completely missed the *social* festive season in Sydney, spending that time away on their honeymoon, maybe they could start off well, celebrating Zack's first Christmas together, feeling like a family.

She desperately wanted to hold onto her dream, believe in it…if only for a little while.

Nick did not move. His mind was locked in battle with his natural instincts. Yes, this marriage was about Tess and Zack but he wasn't into sneaking off to do anything. It went totally against his grain. To his mind, a man wasn't a man if he didn't stand up to be counted.

It was bad enough that Tess had hidden the fact of giving birth to his son, denying him the chance to stand by her. He wanted to ensure that everyone who had any contact with their lives was left in no doubt that he was proud to have Tess as his wife and the mother of his child.

A wedding was a public statement.

That was what it should be.

Yet Tess was acting so skittishly about it, Nick was forced to do a swift reappraisal of his priorities. She'd whirled herself over to the set of French doors which opened onto the side verandah, and she stood there looking out, her arms tightly folded, her back turned to him…clearly a stance of brick-wall revulsion to participating in what she foresaw as *a three-ring circus*.

In his mind's eye, he could see Tess as such a spectacular, incandescent bride, she would absolutely obliterate the stardom of their prima donna mothers. There would be no competition at all. From anyone. Nevertheless, argument on that point looked highly futile at the moment and getting married was the whole object of this exercise.

In fact, given this current display of fraught nerves, best he waste no time at all in getting Zack and Tess legally tied to him. 'We could get on a plane, fly to Las Vegas, come home married—*fait accompli*—if that's how you want it,' he put forward, testing her attitude.

Her head jerked in negation. 'Las Vegas is tacky. Besides...' Her shoulder blades sharpened, signalling a strong wave of inner tension. '...I think it best we wait the month required by Australian law. It is some safeguard against marrying in haste and repenting at leisure.'

Was she having second thoughts or thinking he might have them? 'I won't change my mind, Tess,' he asserted.

She threw him a hard, measuring glance over her shoulder. 'You've hardly been tested by baby demands yet. How do I know you won't run from them, Nick? How do I know you won't leave the major parenting to me once you find out it's not all fun and games?'

'You want the month to see how I stand up to it?'

'One night does not a father make,' she tossed at him.

'I am very personally aware of that,' he shot back. 'If I have one prime aim in life, it's to give my son everything *I* wanted from the father who wasn't there for me.'

'Good intentions don't always stick.'

'They're not intentions. They're vows I'll live by.'

Her eyes mocked his claim. 'My life has been littered with broken promises.'

'Is that why you want a private wedding, Tess? Eas-

ier to call it off? No loss of face if no one knows
about it?'

'That works both ways. You might get bored with
both of us.'

'No chance.'

He shifted off the desk and moved up behind her,
hating the power she still had to limit his connection
to her life and Zack's. He had to erase her doubts
about his commitment, melt the staunchly held independence he sensed was gaining ground again, build
up a need for him, stoke the desire that could override
every other consideration.

He slid his arms around her waist and drew her back
against him. She wore figure-hugging, sexy blue jeans
and as he fitted her lushly curved bottom to his groin,
her rigidity broke under a wave of little tremors. Even
so, her arms remained defensively folded across the
white singlet top, denying him easy access to her sen-
sational breasts. He bent his head to nudge aside the
rioting mass of red ringlets so he could play erotic
games with the delicate shell of her ear, wanting to
win back the soft, pliant, sensual woman who'd shared
her bed with him last night.

'A month of nights won't even begin to satisfy all
you stir in me, Tess,' he murmured, blowing softly
into her ear.

Her whole body shuddered with pleasure, whipping
him into instant arousal. Her arms loosened, dropping
to her sides and moving backwards to claw her hands
up and down his thighs, inciting an even more urgent
desire, matching his erotic move with her own.
Compelled to challenge her for dominant sexual
power, Nick thrust his hands up beneath her singlet

and took possession of her breasts, his own fingers seductively kneading, not clawing.

'We should save something special for our wedding night,' she said, lifting her shoulders back to raise her breasts in proud defiance of his ownership, though the husky edge of her voice betrayed her excitement in it.

'Tell me what would please you?' he urged, purring his own wicked pleasure in the double-edged question. 'How do you envisage our wedding day...and night?'

'Private...beautiful...'

The lilt in her voice started off her siren song again. The need—the desire—to have sex with *this* woman was totally obsessive. 'You want private, you'd better shut the French doors in front of you, Tess,' he said gruffly, dropping one hand down to unclip the waist-band of her jeans. 'As for beautiful, you'll make our wedding beautiful regardless of where we are and what ceremony you choose.'

'There's a place up in far north Queensland...'

'Fine! Book it!' Stud undone, zipper undone, heat uncontainable. 'Shut the doors, Tess!'

One month later Nick was looking at another set of closed doors, waiting for his bride to appear. He'd respected Tess's wish for a completely private wedding—not a whisper to the media about where or when—but she'd certainly stunned him with her choice of place.

He'd felt it wrong that she'd shunned the traditional fairy-tale wedding which should have been detailed with every last scrap of high society trimmings. In a way, it seemed she was cheated out of it by family that had taken a lot from both of them and should be made to go through a few days' pain for Tess's sake, acknowledging her right to be a princess bride.

Yet the moment he'd seen this chapel, Nick had understood that Tess did not feel short-changed by the wedding *she* had arranged. This was the ultimate in romantic fantasy and to Nick's mind, uniquely suited to her.

It was a beautiful little chapel, built in the grounds of a Great Barrier Reef Resort located near Cairns in far north Queensland. Three sides of it were virtually walls of glass; the end wall looking directly out on a white sand beach and a clear turquoise sea, the side walls giving a view of green lawns, palm trees and tropical gardens. Only the wall housing the arched entrance doors was solid, blocking out the sight of other buildings, ensuring that those inside the chapel had this glorious, pristine piece of the world to themselves.

There was no strip of red carpet bisecting the four rows of white pews. Unbelievably the aisle was the glass surface of an underground aquarium, artistically lit to highlight the fantastic shapes and colours of living coral with a horde of tiny tropical fish darting in and out of it. The effect was amazing, giving one the feeling of walking on the sea.

A professional wedding celebrant—a guy in his early fifties with a benevolent, fatherly look about him—stood with Nick, awaiting the bride. To their left were two women in sparkling aqua green dresses— one a pianist seated at a white baby grand piano, the other a singer standing beside her. To the right was a white table, holding a magnificent arrangement of flowers to one side and the official papers to be signed with individual gold pens on the other.

A bell was rung from somewhere outside, obviously

the signal to start proceedings. Nick had been burning with impatience for this moment, wanting the waiting over. It had been a long month, carrying the acute sense of having to prove himself worthy of Tess's consideration as a husband for her, as well as a father for Zack. He wanted the chapel doors to open now, wanted the ceremony over and done with, the marriage certificate signed, sealed and delivered.

The pianist began playing the opening chords to Schubert's *Ave Maria* and as the chapel doors were finally opened, the singer gave full vibrant voice to the traditional hymn, heralding in the bride.

Ave, indeed, Nick thought, feeling completely blown away at the sight of Tess, magnificently gowned in white lace beaded with shimmering threads of tiny crystals. A frothy veil attached to a sparkling tiara adorned her glorious hair which shone with the golden-red fire of the sun, making her look like a goddess of the sea as she walked slowly down the amazing aisle towards him.

A goddess…bringing the gift of life to him…not carrying a bouquet of flowers, but the child they had created together, the living symbol of their union and the pivotal hope for a different life *for* him and *with* him…Zack!

And Nick realised in that moment how absolutely right this wedding was—just the three of them, an intimate entwinement of lives that were about to be legally joined. The only other people here were professionals performing a service run by a highly professional wedding company—outsiders who came cleanly into this hour that belonged solely to Tess and him and Zack, then went cleanly out of it, having contributed what was needed and wanted.

It was strange how deeply moved he was by this personal and private choice. His heart seemed to turn over as Tess reached him and offered Zack to him to hold while the marriage ceremony took place. Her lovely blue eyes seemed to be transmitting an intensely vulnerable hope that this bonding would prove good and true.

The words, 'Trust me,' spilled straight from Nick's mind and off his tongue as he took their son in his arms. It won a wobbly smile from Tess, a sheen of emotional tears making huge blue pools of her eyes. Nick wasn't sure this meant she accepted his word or only wished she could believe in it.

Zack had no doubts, giving a happy, confident gurgle at the exchange of parental control. He'd learnt to trust his father over the past month and Nick privately swore he'd never knowingly let his son down on anything important to him. Trust between adults was a far more complex equation and he hoped Tess accepted that he took today's formal commitment to each other very seriously.

It wasn't a paper marriage to him.

He might have thought of it like that before he'd known about Zack, but this baby in his arms made a world of difference, and Tess, having given birth to his son, took a far more special place in his life, as well. Because of this, instead of throwing up a cynical shield to the words being spoken by the marriage celebrant, Nick found himself listening to them, appreciating the truths behind them.

'This union then is most serious, because it will bind you together for life in a relationship so close and intimate, it will profoundly influence your whole future. That future with its hopes and disappointments, its successes and its failures, its pleasures and its pains, its joys and its sorrows, is hidden from your eyes. You know these elements are mingled in every life and are to be expected in your own...'

Except once married couples hit the bad side of the scales these days, most people didn't go the distance. It took real commitment to stick in there and work things through. The determination to do it welled up in Nick. No way was his child going to be a victim of divorce!

This father is going to play the game straight, Zack, he beamed at his son.

'And so,' the celebrant continued, 'not knowing what is before you, you take each other for better or for worse, for richer or for poorer, in sickness and in health, until death. Truly then, these words are most serious, and it is a beautiful tribute to your undoubted faith in each other, that recognising their full import, you are willing and ready to pronounce them.'

He bestowed an approving smile on the two of them and asked them to join hands, nodding to Nick first as he proceeded with the ceremony. 'Please repeat after me...'

Listening to Nick repeat the old marriage vows in a solemn tone—with no hesitation nor the slightest hint of cynical humour—was precisely what Tess needed to feed the hope that somehow this marriage would be held together.

The celebrant had shown her many modern variations of the marriage service, giving different versions of speeches that could be made by the bride and groom. They were prettily dressed up with pleasing promises, but what they boiled down to was signing up for a partnership contract that would only be kept as long as conditions remained agreeable.

Tess had deliberately chosen the traditional lifelong commitment vows, not consulting Nick over them since he'd given her free rein on making all the decisions about their wedding. They conveyed what *she* wanted, what *she* wished with all her heart, and she felt her heart swelling with a wild joy in Nick's sombre recitation of them.

While he could merely be giving an appropriate performance, the hand holding hers seemed to be transmitting genuine feeling, reinforcing the warm assurance pulsing through his voice. Rightly or wrongly, it imbued her with a happy confidence as she spoke herself, a confidence secretly bolstered by the knowledge she would never break these vows. To her they were very real, and if they weren't real for Nick…she didn't want to know.

When they were finally pronounced 'Husband and wife,' the kiss they shared felt like a kiss of love to Tess…tender, caring, the sweet caress of souls touching and entwining in recognition of belonging together. Whether it was her own deep need fuelling pure fantasy she couldn't tell, but as they moved on to the table to put their signatures to this marriage, the lyrics being sung by the wedding singer about always remembering these feelings and never letting them end found instant echoes in her mind.

CHAPTER NINE

'WHAT'S going on, Tessa?' her father demanded, his sharp blue gaze assessing her new home as she ushered him through it to the patio overlooking Sydney Harbour. 'I heard Nick Ramirez snapped this property up when it came on the market a month or so ago. Paid fifteen million for it.'

'Yes, he did,' she agreed, anxiously wondering if this get-together *here* for morning tea was the best lead-in to the news she had to impart.

'So how much did he take off you to sell it on?' Her father's tone was both belligerent and suspicious, hating the idea that Nick might have ripped off his daughter on a property deal. 'Not that it would be a bad buy in any event,' he added, not wanting to demean her business sense. 'Dress circle location at Point Piper. Can't go wrong with it. But it's a hell of a quick turnover from him to you.'

'It wasn't like that, Dad,' she stated quietly.

Shaggy white eyebrows beetled down. 'What are you saying? He was fronting for you in buying this place?'

'Well, yes. He bought it for me. And Zack. As a home for us.'

'Why use him?'

Tess's heart sank at the distaste and disapproval in his voice.

'If you wanted to employ an agent to buy you a new home...'

112

'Dad, please stop,' she begged. 'I just want to show you…'

'Okay…okay…' He held up a hand, halting himself from any further outpouring of prejudice from past personal circumstances. He swept his gaze around some more. 'It's a fine house, Tessa.'

At last they stepped out onto the patio facing a view that swept right down the wide expanse of middle harbour to the opera house at Bennelong Point and beyond, with Sydney's huge coathanger bridge forming a fabulous backdrop. It was a beautiful sunny morning, blue sky, sparkling water, and Tess desperately wanted her father to be warmly influenced by positive elements.

'Going to need quite a few staff to maintain all this for you,' he observed, gesturing to the grounds which had been terraced down to the foreshore; beautifully manicured lawns and perfectly planned gardens sweeping out from the patio, a swimming pool surrounded by a colonnaded pavilion on a lower level, a tennis court below that, and finally a boatshed and wharf.

'That's been taken care of, Dad,' she assured him, walking on to the entertainment bar under the side pergola, and waving to the table and chairs she'd set up for their use. 'Sit down and relax while I brew us a pot of tea.'

'Hard to get good reliable people,' he warned, following her to sit on a stool on the other side of the bar while she boiled water for the pot. 'Did you get their credentials vetted properly? Having made the decision to set up home here, you've got to think more about security, Tessa. It's not just you now, you know. There's my grandchild to think of. Not that kidnapping has been a common crime in Australia, but…where is Zack?' He swung around on the stool to look for a pram or some other baby container. 'I was expecting to see him.'

Tess took a deep breath and feeling there really was no way to blunt the shock, simply said, 'Zack is with his father.'

'*Father!*' He swung back very sharply, eyes lasering Tess's for a lot more information than that.

'You advised telling him about his son and I did,' she hastily declared.

'I didn't advise giving up any custodial rights,' was snapped back at her. 'Just who is this guy, Tessa? I thought you said he wouldn't be interested.'

'I was wrong.'

'But Zack is still only a baby. How could you let him out of your care? My grandson…'

'He's not out of my care. We're…we're a family, Dad.' She screwed her courage to the sticking point and blurted out, 'I married Zack's father three weeks ago.'

His jaw dropped in shock.

'I didn't want a big fussy wedding,' she rattled out as quickly as she could. 'We flew up to Cairns and…'

Her father's hands crashed down on the bar counter as he stood up from the stool, his shoulders squaring, his barrel chest puffing out aggressively as he towered up to his full formidable height and thundered, 'You marry some bastard who got you pregnant without letting me get the lawyers onto him first! Where are your brains, Tessa? He took you once and walked away and he'll take you again. Big time!'

'No, he won't!' she retorted with absolute certainty. 'Nick would never take a cent of Steele money. He bought this place for us all by himself. He's paid for everything in it. He's employing the staff, paying their wages. This is all...'

'Nick!' The name exploded from her father's mouth. His neck and face went bright red. 'Are you telling me you've married Nick Ramirez? That *he's* Zack's father? Is this what you're telling me, Tessa?'

'Yes, I am.' Her chin came up in proud defiance of any criticism of her personal judgement.

He shook his head in rank incredulity. 'I don't believe it!' He turned his back on her as though confirmation would be too painful to confront. 'I can't believe it!'

'Nick is good with Zack, Dad,' Tess pleaded. 'Very good.'

He wheeled around, arms flying out, hands clenched to punch out his points. 'Marrying Nick Ramirez is setting yourself up for one humiliation after another,' he cried in anguished protest at her decision. 'He might not be a gigolo bleeding you of money, but I've heard he's into the pants of every beautiful woman who walks through his life. *Just like his father.*'

Hate-filled words, loaded with his own humiliation at the hands of Enrique Ramirez.

Tess frantically sought a way to counter them, her stomach churning over the very real possibility of a unbridgeable rift with her father opening up. She couldn't deny Nick's personal history and it was impossible to claim the future would be any different, yet she burned with the need to believe in the sense of unity she felt she had achieved with him in the past seven weeks.

'At least Zack will know I married his father,' she said fiercely. 'He'll know I tried to set up a family home and life for him. And if it fails, he'll still have—he'll always have—a mother who not only loves him but will always have time for him.'

Tears welled into her eyes and her throat choked up as memories of how deeply and frequently her own mother had failed in giving her either time or caring when it was sorely needed. There had been so many emotional *holes* in her life and maybe Nick wouldn't fill them. Maybe he'd leave them emptier than ever in the end. But right now…

The electric kettle started a shrill whistle and she reached blindly for the switch. In the few seconds it took to find it and click it off, her father had rounded the counter of the bar and she found herself wrapped in a tight hug, her back being patted as though she were a baby needing comfort. Which she did.

'It's okay…okay. You've got a father, Tessa,' he gruffly assured her. 'No matter what happens with Nick Ramirez, you just remember you've got a father to turn to.'

The knotted tension inside her started unravelling. Tess's whole body sagged in relief. Her father was not going to storm away. He cared enough to stay for her, and the proven magnitude of that caring caused the tears to flow unchecked,

'I'm sorry you had it so rough as a kid, Tessa.' His big chest rose and fell in a long, ragged sigh. 'Damned difficult situation. I tried to even it out. Didn't do too well, I guess.'

He hadn't done too badly, Tess thought, given Livvy's capricious temperament and his third wife's jealousy. She held no grudge against her father for his part in her life. 'You've always done good, Dad,' she managed to choke out.

'You should have let me give you a proper wedding,' he said, a touch of wounded pride coming to the fore. 'My only daughter…it should have been the biggest and best damned wedding money could buy.'

Tess sucked in a deep breath and lifted her head back to speak directly to him, gathering all her mental strength to keep her voice from wobbling. 'You can't buy people's feelings, Dad. *Damned wedding* says it in a nutshell. You would have hated handing me over to Nick and your three wives would have been at each other's throats…'

He grimaced at that undeniable truth.

'Much better to keep it small and private—just me and Nick and Zack.'

'Zack…' His mouth slowly twisted up into a wry smile. 'Guess I got stuck with my own advice.'

'It was the right advice, Dad. It turned out well.'

He searched her eyes worriedly. 'Did it, Tessa? Never mind Zack. I mean for you. God knows you've been short-changed of love all your life. Marrying for the sake of a child…'

'No!' She shook her head vehemently. 'Don't think that, Dad. Nick and I…we do have something good going together…'

Sex! Fantastic, addictive, incredibly wonderful sex! And lots of it! But she couldn't say that to her father and a self-conscious blush was heating up her cheeks even as she thought it.

'I wouldn't have married him if I hadn't…*wanted* him as my husband.'

'*Wanted*…' The tone of voice and the derisive flash in the blue eyes knew precisely what she was referring to in relation to Nick Ramirez.

It shamed Tess into revealing the truth in her heart.

'I love him, Dad. I have from the very beginning. And I'm going to take all I can have of him. Please…try to understand and go along with me?'

'Oh, I understand, Tessa.' He lifted a hand to her cheek and gently rubbed at the wet stain of tears as his eyes shared a moment of mocking reflection with her. 'We grab what we can of what feels good. That's what makes life worth living.'

Tess wasn't sure that was her philosophy, but she could see it was his…*take, but expect to pay a price, because nothing comes free*. It was part of the corruption that came with great wealth. Love was above that, she argued to herself. It was a gift that couldn't be bought. But it could be paid for in pain, a little voice in her mind warned.

'Let's get this kettle boiled again,' her father directed, releasing her from his embrace. 'We could both do with a cup of tea.'

It was a huge relief that their usual father/daughter harmony had been re-established and Tess was grateful for some normal activity to bridge the awkwardness of having released so much naked emotion. The tea was quickly made and she carried the pot over to the table where her father had finally seated himself.

'Have you told your mother about your marriage?' he asked.

'Not yet. She's off touring at the moment and we've only just returned from our honeymoon. Nick wants to hold a big celebration party once we've got this house in order. I'll break it to her before the invitations go out.'

'Bound to create a sensation the moment you go public on it.'

'Yes, but it shouldn't last long. And it's easier to ride with a *fait accompli*, don't you think?'

'What's done is done,' he intoned dryly. 'And since we've now had our private *tête-à-tête*, where is your husband with my grandson?'

She heard the belligerent note edging his voice again and sensed it heralded a demand for a face to face meeting with Nick who had insisted on the same thing, conceding her only half an hour alone with her father before he barged in on them. The image of two bulls locking horns agitated her mind as she glanced nervously towards the flight of steps leading down from the garden level to the pool terrace.

Her gaze was caught and held by Nick's head rising into view as he mounted the steps—his shoulders, then Zack in the carry pouch harnessed to his father's chest, little baby legs happily kicking, Nick smiling down at him, having the usual one-sided conversation he had with their son, which Zack adored, lapping up being the focus of loving vocal attention.

'He cares about his son,' came the gruff observation from her father.

'Very much.'

'And you, Tessa…' The tone sharpened. '…how much does he care about you?'

She hesitated, not wanting to sound negative, yet having no real knowledge of the answer. 'More than I expected,' she said. 'He keeps…surprising me.' Which was absolutely true.

But she was very much on tenterhooks again as Nick approached, the good humour on his face fading into a tense *on guard* look, green eyes watching and acutely assessing the body language of the man whose financial power and influential connections could become a force to be reckoned with in their lives.

Her father pushed back his chair, rose to his feet, and for her sake—Tess knew—moved to make peace, not war, thrusting out his hand for Nick to take if he was willing.

'You no longer carry my name,' he started, referring to the eighteen years before the surname of Steele was legally changed to Ramirez. 'I respect the integrity behind publicly correcting that lie and proclaiming your true bloodline. However, my daughter tells me you are now my son-in-law, the father of my grandson, and those two circumstances unquestionably makes you family. Right?'

'Right!' Nick affirmed, grasping the offered hand and eyeballing her father with a charge of dynamic energy that encompassed all of them as he added, 'And let it be clear we would have been family much sooner if Tess had told me she was pregnant with my child.'

Her father nodded an acknowledgement that truth was being spoken on that point, too, though he very deliberately posed the question—'Difficult situation when choices seem…forced…don't you think?'

The reply was instant. 'I don't blame Tess for the decisions she made. Given her viewpoint, she had just cause for them, though I would have told her differently, given the chance. I deeply regret that I wasn't at her side, sharing what should have been shared.'

'I'd like to think you were up for it,' her father said testingly. 'Don't know if she told you but Tessa had a real bad time giving birth. Damned doctors were slow to act on a Caesarean in my opinion. Put stress

on Tessa and on Zack. Then getting an infection from
the operation...'

'Dad, that's over,' Tess broke in insistently, seeing
Nick's face tightening up and frightened of any threat
to the rather fragile peace-making.

'Yes, she did tell me,' Nick bit out, ignoring her
interruption as he concentrated unrelentingly on her
father. 'You have my respect...and deep gratitude...for answering her needs, for ensuring Tess was
not alone while she was giving birth to my child. You
were there for her, supporting her, and I thank you for
it very sincerely.'

'She's my daughter...'

'And now my wife,' Nick sliced back, his voice
gathering a fierce vehemence as he went on. 'Believe
me...you will not be required to sit in my place again.'
He withdrew his hand from her father's clasp to curl
it possessively around Zack. 'Nor will you be required
to stand in for me any time in the future where my
wife or son is concerned.'

Pride blazed from him and Tess held her breath as
her father's eyes narrowed, denying pride any power
whatsoever.

'Make good on those words, Nick Ramirez, and
you'll never have a quarrel with me,' he punched out.

'I am not my father, Brian Steele. Don't make the
mistake of dressing me with his character,' came the
swift counter-stroke. 'I took his name because it belonged to me, but I am my own man and one thing
you can be absolutely certain of...I will always fight
for what belongs to me.'

'So will I. I wouldn't forget who your wife is, if I
were you.'

'Dad...' Tess leapt to her feet, her hands begging

her father to listen, to hear, to realise… 'Threats won't make good things happen. Don't do this. Please? It's my choice, my risk, my life…'

'*Our* life!' Nick sharply corrected, moving to put his free arm around her shoulders and tuck her right next to him. 'Tess and I are working it out together. We have a child. We're going to make a good home, be a family. You can be part of it…'

'Please, Dad?' Tess leapt in, her heart hammering with a wild, joyful hope in the powerful flow of emotion pouring from Nick. 'Let it be good?'

Her father heaved a big sigh, visibly putting aside the suspicions and animosity. He gave Nick a challenging glare then dropped his gaze to the table. 'Cup of tea would have gone cold by now,' he growled. 'And I haven't even had a nurse of my grandson. Better start making good on that…both of you. I get invited over here and all you're giving me is aggravation.'

As fast as the tension had escalated between the two men, it eased. Her father slid into a conversation about acquiring property. Nick joined him in sitting down at the table, contributing to the neutral topic while gently lifting Zack out of the carry pouch and passing him over to his grandfather.

Intensely grateful for the truce, Tess left them to establishing a safe meeting ground while she retreated behind the bar to boil a fresh lot of water. After being caught up in a strong swirl of primitive male undercurrents—paternal protection and husband staking *his* claims—it was with a sense of almost hysterical relief that she now played her part in the highly civilised activity of serving morning tea.

Fortunately, both these important men in her life

had the self-control and intelligence to avoid an irre-pairable situation, though Tess was aware of consid-erable testing and weighing being carried on behind their seemingly innocuous exchange of ideas and opin-ions. Certainly, neither of them was about to withdraw from this engagement, giving ground to his opponent, and respect was eventually granted, though Tess sensed it was hedged around with a lot of provisions relating to how the future was handled.

Which, she readily conceded, was only reasonable. She had her own doubts about how far Nick's com-mitment to her would extend. Their marriage currently hinged on fatherhood and sex and both factors still had their novelty to Nick. While she did believe he would always be there for his son, his sexual affairs had never lasted long. To her knowledge, six months at most. After that...

She instantly put a mental block on looking too far ahead. As yet, Nick had given her no reason to fear any break up of their marriage and she wasn't about to present any hint of uncertainty about its future to her father. Today, at least, she wanted to present a solid front with Nick.

'Looking at Zack...and you...' Her father shot a sardonic look at Nick. '...couldn't have been any doubt in *your* mind that you're his father.'

'No. Though I would have believed Tess's word even if Zack had favoured her in looks,' Nick rolled back at him.

'As I did, your mother,' came the mocking remem-brance.

Tess tensed, anticipating a swift return to crossing swords.

Nick shook his head. 'There is no comparison between my mother and Tess,' he said quietly. 'Their hearts are in very different places.'

Her father grunted a grudging approval. 'Good that you're aware of it.'

'And while I appreciate that Zack's birth was very difficult for her,' Nick ran on, 'should Tess ever feel up to going through with another pregnancy...'

'You *want* us to have another child?' she leapt in, elation whipping up a surge of happiness at this plan for their future.

'Neither your mother nor mine provided us with a brother or sister, Tess,' he pointed out. 'I think we were both lonely children.'

'Yes,' she quickly agreed.

Nick's mesmerisingly magnetic green eyes searched hers warily, not wanting to apply pressure yet unable to stop an eloquent appeal from shining through. 'I'd like us to do better for Zack.'

'We will.'

The promise tripped straight off her tongue, accompanied by a brilliantly joyous smile that instantly demolished any further note of discord from her father. Or if there was one during the rest of his visit, Tess didn't hear it. She heard only the hope singing in her heart.

Nick had just surprised her again.

Another child...proving a deep commitment to their marriage...ongoing partners in creating life and sharing in it.

Tess added this good feeling to all the other good feelings Nick had given her. It had to be getting close to love. Or maybe she was colouring *the surprises* with her own love.

Whatever...life with Nick was good.

And getting better every day.

CHAPTER TEN

THE invitation to breakfast with his mother *at home* meant she wanted something from him. The messages she'd been persistently leaving for him over the past three weeks had told Nick she had some issue on her mind that required his attention and ignoring it was not going to make it go away. Besides which, now that Brian Steele knew about his marriage to Tess, it was probably best to break the news privately to the new mother-in-law, as well.

One thing was certain. He didn't want Tess anywhere near his mother until he'd dealt with the initial reaction, which would inevitably shoot out a host of bad vibrations, making Tess feel even more vulnerable about their marriage. As it was, she didn't trust him to keep to his commitment.

My risk, she'd fired at her father.

And she'd looked stunned at the suggestion that they have another child—stunned but happy that he was planning so much of a future with her—which implied she thought of their relationship as a temporary one on *his* part, though clearly not on hers. She expected him to stray. After all, a long string of temporary relationships had been the pattern of his life— his whole life—and they hadn't been together long enough for her to believe this marriage would be any different.

Though it was.

Hugely different to anything Nick had known before.

He wasn't about to lose it or have it damaged by people who didn't understand where he was with Tess and what he felt with her and Zack. Tess had warded off any threat of damage by her father yesterday, standing firmly by her *choice* to marry him. It was up to him this morning to ensure damage didn't come their way from his mother.

Breakfast in the Condor residence was held in a brilliant sunny room, decorated in buttercup-yellow and white, the table situated to take full advantage of the view over Balmoral Beach and the marina where Philip Condor kept his yacht.

The housekeeper ushered Nick into it. His mother, of course, was gracefully posed on a chair turned to half-face where he would enter, so he was given the full impact of the figure-hugging chartreuse slacks— the perfect curve of hip and thigh denying the slightest dimple of cellulite—matched with a tied at the waist floral blouse in chartreuse, white and lemon, showing off the top-end female ammunition.

'Darling!' She rose from her chair with a fluid sex-iness that had probably been practised a million times, giving him pouty air kisses on both cheeks before tucking her arm around his in a cosy hug and leading him to the chair at the head of the table—*the man's* place. 'Where have you been?' she chided prettily, her fingers busily stroking to get under his skin.

It reminded Nick of what a very *straight* pleasure it was to live with Tess who never played these little power games. He could not recall her ever triggering the kind of cynical double thinking he did around his mother. Indeed, around all the women who'd paraded through his life. Except Tess. Who'd made a practice of always dealing directly, not attempting to oil her way anywhere.

Still, he had to concede Tess had never done without financially—an heiress to a fortune from the day she was born. Nadia Kilman had been the only child of very poor immigrants to Australia—people who'd striven hard to give their beautiful daughter every possible advantage in their new country, only to be cheated of revelling in her glory, both of them dying while trying to save their home on the outskirts of Sydney from a summer firestorm.

Of course, they'd ensured Nadia was safe first. Nadia, at sixteen, had already begun a shining future as a model. Her rags to riches background had served her well, too, drawing admiration and generating sympathetic chances for her to advance. And advance. And advance. No looking back for Nadia Kilman. Looking forward was much more to her liking.

'You've got me here now, Mother,' Nick stated dryly. 'What's on your mind?'

Probably best to play her game first, get her in a good mood.

'Juice? Coffee?' Ready to play serving maid, which undoubtedly meant she wanted a big favour from him! After all, he was only her son, not a billionaire marriage prospect.

'I'll help myself, thank you.'

A complete breakfast buffet was laid out. He poured himself a long glass of freshly squeezed orange juice and took a croissant to help pass the time in a civil manner. They both settled at the table, his mother projecting immense pleasure in his company.

'You bought the Upton place at Point Piper!' came

the opening line, the gold-amber eyes sparkling delight in the acquisition.

'Yes. I heard it was to be put on the market and did a private deal,' he answered matter-of-factly.

'I've been to so many wonderful parties there! Though I must say, neither the Uptons nor the Farrells before them ever made the most of that marvellous house. Now what I'd like to suggest, Nick—and you know how good I am at this—instead of getting in some professional interior decorator...'

'No. Don't go there, Mother,' he warned. 'The position is already taken.'

'But I *need* a new project.' She pouted and smiled, playing all her appealing tricks. 'And I'd give you a brilliant result. I promise your new home will be the talk of the town. Let me pay off whatever contract you've signed...'

'No. This is not a negotiable situation.'

'Darling, *everything* is negotiable. It's just a matter of finding the right price.'

Nick shook his head, realising he would have made the same cynical generalisation only a few weeks ago, but he knew now that wasn't true. The love he felt towards his son wasn't negotiable. And the trust he wanted Tess to feel with him wasn't negotiable. In fact, nothing relating to either Zack or Tess was negotiable.

'I know you like to do things your own way,' his mother ran on, 'but you have to concede that I have huge expertise in...'

He waved a sharp dismissal of any persuasive tactics and stated bluntly, 'I've married since I saw you last. My wife will be choosing and overseeing whatever decoration she wants done in our home.'

'Married!' She stared at him in stunned disbelief. When he didn't repudiate his statement, disbelief moved to chagrin. 'Why haven't I heard of this?'

'Well, basically it's none of your business,' Nick answered evenly, shrugging away any criticism as he added, 'I don't recall you ever consulting me on any of your marriages. You just went ahead...'

'You knew *who* I was marrying,' she broke in, more angry at having her own plans frustrated than caring about his choice of wife.

'Irrelevant, Mother. The point is...'

'I want to know who,' she cut in petulantly. 'After all your cynical cracks about my marriages, I want to know who and what changed your mind about giving marriage a try yourself. It's so totally out of character...'

'You may have misjudged my character.'

The thought burned through his mind again... *I am not my father!*

She rolled her eyes. 'Just give me her name. I'll judge for myself where you're coming from, Nick.'

He felt a quiet sense of pride as he said, 'Tessa Steele is now my wife.'

'Tessa Steele?' His mother's voice climbed, gathering a shrill edge. 'Tessa Steele—Brian Steele's daughter?'

He nodded.

She broke into a wild peal of laughter. 'Oh, that's priceless! Absolutely priceless!' she spluttered, standing up and pirouetting around, clapping her hands in girlish glee. 'Brian gets rid of me as his wife and you get his one and only daughter to marry you! I love it!'

Nick sighed in sheer exasperation at her habit of turning everything back to herself. Just for once, he wished she could move beyond the centre of her own universe.

Her arms lifted, hands reaching out to gloatingly gather in and express what his marriage to Tess meant to her. 'It has such delicious symmetry! And all that lovely money is back in the family! What a glorious, fabulous coup!'

Money!

Nick's jaw clenched as he fought back a tumultuous wave of hatred for the values his mother had espoused all her life...the sheer meanness of it in human terms.

'Nothing on this earth would induce me to take one cent of the Steele family fortune,' he grated.

His mother was momentarily dumbfounded by this emphatic claim, but she quickly rallied, scoffing, 'Then why marry her? She's not even beautiful.'

'She is to me.' He stood up, too angry to remain seated. 'And more to the point, Tess has had my child—a son...'

'A child!' she spat, rolling her eyes at the supposed idiocy of his decisions. 'So, the boot is on the other foot and you fell for it. She used that trap to get you to marry her, just as I did, Brian.'

'No, Mother. Not as you did, Brian. I wasn't his son, whereas Zack is definitely mine.'

'You have proof of that?'

'Indisputable.'

'Well, it was damned clever of her, anyway. No doubt she guessed you had a thing about being rejected by your father. And having a boy-baby...perfect weapon to pull you in.'

Anger was pulsing from both of them and the conversation was fast escalating into a vicious row because his mother had decided her side wasn't winning any more and she had no understanding of the stakes in play and probably never would.

Nick took a deep breath to calm himself down and quietly corrected her view. 'Tess didn't use it to pull me in. In fact, she didn't even reveal our son's existence until *after* I'd proposed marriage to her.'

'What?'

'You heard me. I proposed marriage first.'

'Why?'

'Because I wanted to. Because I wanted exactly what Tess and Zack are now giving me.'

'And just when did you decide that, Nick? I know you were still playing the field when Enrique died and that wasn't even two months ago.'

The packet from Brazil...

Weird irony that he had barely given a thought to his father's letter since Tess had told him about Zack, yet what he'd read as his father's fantasy of an ideal life was now shaping up as his reality. Had Enrique got it right at the end? Certainly the carrot of meeting two half-brothers had pushed Nick into considering a marriage with Tess and subsequently acting on the idea, bringing him to where he was now.

'Did the news of your father's death suddenly awaken a sense of mortality in you?' his mother mocked, impatient for a definitive reply from him. 'Time to get married and beget children?' she ran on, determined on pinning him down to her satisfaction.

Which meant fitting his decisions and actions into her values and that was impossible. Nick shook his head, realising he'd moved too far from his mother's standpoint to establish any understanding between them.

'Just go on living your own life, Mother, and let me

live mine,' he said dismissively, holding up a hand in farewell before heading out of her domain.

Far from acknowledging his exit line, her face lit up with the excitement of having seized an insight that answered everything on her terms. 'The inheritance! That's what this marriage is about, isn't it? You denied that Enrique had left you anything but why would he gift me the emerald necklace and not give you—his own son!—much more? Marrying Tessa Steele is your ticket to the Ramirez estate,' she declared triumphantly.

Nick's stomach contracted at the sickening equation.

Her golden eyes narrowed to a satisfied glitter. 'Yes, I can see him laughing as he wrote in the provision,' she ran on. 'A well-rounded joke on life…'

'No, Mother,' Nick bit out in grim fury. 'I won't touch a cent of the Ramirez fortune, either, and you could not be more wrong in linking Tess to a black joke on life by your Brazilian lover. She was not named in my father's letter to me.'

One perfectly plucked eyebrow arched in disbelief. 'Darling, you can trust me to keep a secret.'

It was futile trying to correct her.

She gave her feline smile. 'What exactly did Enrique write to you?'

'I told you,' he said with cold finality. 'He revealed I had two half-brothers—family I didn't know about.'

'And they'd get the inheritance if you didn't…'

'This is not about any inheritance!' he yelled, driven beyond any tolerance for her priorities. 'I came to tell you I had a family of my own now. Though I can see you're not the least bit interested in your grandson, any more than you were ever interested in me.'

'How can you say that?' she protested heatedly.

'Very easily!' He tipped her a savagely mocking salute. 'Good morning to you, Mother! Go ask Philip to buy you another house to decorate. Mine is off limits to you!'

'Off limits?' she screeched after him as he made his exit from the breakfast room, closing the door on *her scene.*

He didn't wait to be shown out of the *showcase* home. He strode out on his own steam, wishing he hadn't bothered coming. The only shared ground he had left with his mother was their past—the mother-son link that had tied them together whether they liked it or not. He'd thought it warranted courtesy but his mother's attitude towards Tess and their marriage precluded that.

This was the parting of the ways.

It was time to let go what had never been good, anyway.

The emptiness there'd always been in his relationship with his mother was being filled by Zack and Tess. He certainly didn't need to hang onto any maternal apron strings.

All this sound reasoning was running through Nick's mind as he drove away from Balmoral Beach. Unhappily, he was not taking into account the fact that his mother might not want to let him go, nor did he consider how frustrated she might be feeling about being thwarted by him on a number of issues.

In fact, Nadia Kilman/Steele/Manning/Hardwick/Condor was deciding on milking another source for the information she wanted—Nick's new convenient wife, who could hardly deny her the right to see her own grandson!

CHAPTER ELEVEN

BY THE time Nadia Condor finally took her leave, Tess felt the bottom had dropped out of her brave new world with Nick and she was free-falling into the most miserable darkness of her life. At least she'd cobbled enough pride together so that Nick's mother could not have realised how much pain she had delivered, but that was little solace for the total shattering of her private fantasy.

The whole black irony was…she'd believed Nick's word that this marriage would never involve them in *the property trap*. He didn't want or need any part of her wealth and she didn't want or need any part of his. It had never occurred to her there could be other property tied to their marriage. She knew nothing of the *fabulous Ramirez estate*. More to the point, Nick had not mentioned his father's death, nor the terms of inheritance.

A marriage of convenience—that was what he had proposed and what she had accepted, *for Zack's sake*, so their son would have a live-in father for as long as Nick was prepared to *live in*. What she had to do now was hold onto that reasoning and move forward as though nothing had changed, because in real terms, nothing had.

They were married.

Nick had bought them this magnificent family home.

He was not only living in, but proving to be a great

father, even wanting them to have another child to-gether—a brother or sister for Zack.

She had no complaints about him as a husband, ei-ther. He was caring, considerate, as generous with the time they spent together as though they truly were lov-ers, and the sex they shared had not lost one iota of its passionate heat. This was as good as she could have expected it to get...given that love had never been declared.

Promising it in his marriage vows didn't count. *She* had chosen the words to be spoken. At the time, his tone of voice had actually persuaded her into thinking he meant them, but no doubt she'd been carried away by the emotional high of the ceremony, no feet on the ground at all.

It had taken Nadia Condor to bring her crashing down to earth today. Loving Nick Ramirez with all her heart did not mean he ever had to love her back. She had to stop feeding herself this fantasy. It was completely out of kilter with Nick's purpose in choos-ing her as his wife...the one woman he could count on not to demand a divorce settlement, which he'd told her upfront!

This terrible grief now ravaging her heart was grief she'd given to herself. Nick hadn't lied to her. He had withheld some highly personal and private motivation for his decision to marry, but he hadn't lied to her. Nor had he seduced her into marriage. He had laid out his plan very reasonably...not offering anything more than a partnership that could serve both of them well. He was fulfilling his part of their partnership.

It was absurd of her to feel deceived.

It was wrong to blame Nick for her own love affair with self-deception.

She would not let Nadia Condor destroy the solidly supportive relationship they had achieved together, starting from the night of revelation when Nick had learnt about their son. His love for Zack was real. And while their marriage might have been conceived for the sake of *financial* convenience—Tess hated that with a deep, dark, savage hatred—she kept telling herself it had progressed to something else.

Something good.

Too good to be messed up by foolish pride.

So when Nick came home from work, she tried not to show any difference inside her, tried to act naturally as they followed their normal evening routine, tried to stay relaxed in both behaviour and conversation. She didn't realise she was a dismal failure. She was trying so hard...

Something was wrong.

Nick couldn't pick up on precisely what it was, but Tess was definitely not her usual self. During the hour before dinner, designated as playtime with Zack before he was put to bed with his bottle, her face did not light up with ready smiles and laughter. No amusing anecdotes of their son's daily activities were offered. She was quiet, seemingly preoccupied, only joining in the fun of playing with Zack when Nick drew her into it, and then he sensed it was an effort for her to take any real pleasure in what they were doing. Her mind seemed elsewhere, not clicking easily with his.

The Karitane nurse she had employed, Carol Tunny, was still with them. Although her expertise with newborn babies was not really required any more, it was good to have her on hand to take care of Zack when both of them were busy. Nick reasoned that it couldn't be any worry over their son that had Tess disturbed. They saw him settled happily for the night in his new cot, and there was no word to Carol about any concern.

Nick threw his arm around Tess's shoulders in a casual hug as they headed downstairs for dinner, wanting to project comforting support if she needed to unload some personal burden onto him. Her back muscles instantly stiffened as though his touch was unwelcome, even offensive!

'Tess?' he queried, frowning at her reaction.

An apologetic smile was flashed and her shoulders sagged loosely as she gave vent to a sigh. 'Long day with people coming and going, leaving me brochures on furniture and fabric samples for curtains and upholstery.'

'Tess, if decisions are stressing you out, just leave the whole interior decorating up to…'

'No, I want to choose. It's *our* home,' she said with passionate emphasis. 'If I leave it to *them*, we'll get the polished, professional, up to the minute trendy outcome that says nothing about us, apart from the fact we've got *the money* to do it.'

Nick suspected that an heiress sore point was burning. 'Has anyone been criticising your decisions? Making you feel…'

'No, no. It's just been a trying day. How was yours?' She shot him a guarded glance. 'You didn't let me know how breakfast with your mother went.'

Damn! That had probably been chewing up her mind! He should have telephoned and given her a report, ensuring she knew the meeting was totally inconsequential. Though Tess should realise that *his* mother's opinion of their marriage would be as irrelevant as *her* mother's opinion—both of them based on the way they lived their own lives.

'Predictably,' he drawled. 'She can't imagine I didn't marry you only for money, any more than I daresay Livvy Curtin can imagine you didn't marry me only for sex. Why else, darling?' he mimicked mockingly.

Tess flashed him an ironic smile. 'Why else, indeed?'

Nick relaxed, thinking how easy it was to communicate with Tess. The nuances from their family backgrounds were instantly recognised and appreciated. Sometimes words weren't even necessary. Just a look conveyed meaning and understanding. One of the best things about their relationship was this sense of togetherness, of so much being truly shared.

'No joy in being told she has a grandson,' he added. 'No doubt Zack is solid evidence of her aging. I don't foresee much social contact between us from now on.'

'You don't mind losing a mother?'

'Did I ever have one?'

'She has been…a central figure in your life, Nick.'

'Difficult not to be when she was the only blood relation who laid claim to me, which could hardly be evaded once I'd been used to snag your father into marriage. That was very public motherhood. Undeniable. So possession had to be maintained, didn't it?'

His mind drifted to his other blood relations—his unknown half-brothers—wondering what situations they had been born into—how their mothers had *explained* their pregnancies. If Enrique had claimed them as his sons at all, Nick had little doubt that it had been done after he was dead, not before.

They might have been adopted out, or led to believe other men were their fathers, as he had once believed Brian Steele was his. In which case, the news from Brazil could well be causing as much upheaval in their lives as had eventuated for him.

'Possessions can be important to people,' Tess commented wryly.

'They certainly are to my mother,' Nick answered with feeling, frowning over her avid fixation on the Ramirez estate. He didn't care if it went to his half-brothers. It might make a positive difference in their lives. A wonderful windfall. To him, it would always be tainted—a death-gift, not a life-gift. He had no need of it and he wanted no part of it.

'Well, Nadia did know what it was like to be without when she was a child, Nick,' Tess reminded him. 'You and I have never been *in that place*.'

True. Because of his mother's ambitious machinations he had been born to wealth and privilege, just like Tess. He didn't know what *need* was in any material sense so it was all too easy for him to overlook what was behind his mother's drive to acquire the riches of this world. Maybe to her, one could never have enough.

'She's always looking for more,' he muttered as they entered the dining-room. 'Even this morning she wanted to get her hands on this house, decorating it to give herself a buzz and get more admiration from people with her achievement. She doesn't understand the word, *home*. Everything is a showcase for her.'

'What does *home* mean to you?' Tess asked in a quiet, testing tone that struck another wrong note with Nick.

He swung her into a full embrace, one arm gathering her close as he lifted a hand to her face where the signs of inner tension were all too evident…her lovely blue eyes clouded, her gaze flickering from his, seeking evasion. He cupped her cheek to command her attention.

'The old adage is true, Tess. *Home is where the heart is.* And my heart is here with you and Zack,' he said, intently watching her response.

'Right!' She flashed a bright smile…all teeth, not reaching her eyes—and whirled out of his embrace, waving her arms at the dining-room suite which had been brought from his Woolloomooloo apartment. The table was glass, set on slabs of black marble and the black leather chairs from Italy were the latest modern style. 'Then you won't mind if I throw out this stark furniture and replace it with a lovely soft apple-green arrangement because my heart isn't into black. I don't want darkness. I don't want…'

'Apple-green sounds great!' he quickly assured her, hearing an almost frantic note in her voice. 'By all means, throw this furniture out. It was only meant as a stop-gap until we made other choices.'

Although the top end of the table where he stood was set for dinner, the far end was strewn with brochures and fabric samples, and Tess headed for them, snatching up some as she effectively put the whole length of the table between them.

'I'd like you to take a look at these. But open the bottle of chardonnay first.' She gestured to the ice-bucket—wine selected and ready for them. 'We're having a chicken-and-chorizo hot pot, cook tells me. She'll probably be serving it any minute now. Might as well pour the wine.'

Something was very wrong, Nick decided.

Evasive tactics were being employed, both verbal and physical, and he could feel Tess's emotional detachment from him. Barriers were being put up again. Nick didn't know why but he knew where they could best be smashed.

He was not about to tolerate any barriers in the bedroom.

Tess sat at the dressing-table in the master bedroom, brushing her hair, trying to calm her inner agitation with the steady, repetitive action. She had her own furniture around her here, having brought it from her home in Randwick. It didn't suit this house—this room—but at least it gave her the comfortable sense of familiarity.

She'd put on a wrap-around robe, a blue silk and lace negligee which was part of a lingerie set she'd bought for their honeymoon. It was designed to look alluring, but seduction was not on her agenda tonight. She'd felt too vulnerable for the uninhibited nakedness Nick had encouraged in their bedroom, though the robe was not so much to hide her nakedness but to take away the chill of it. It was mid-summer and the air-conditioning in the house was adapted to summer temperatures, yet goose-bumps kept shivering over her skin.

She wished she could feel the heat of desire building up in her, anticipating the intimacies to come in the bed Nick expected her to share with him tonight. For better or for worse, he was her husband, and as he'd said himself, great sex was the glue that made marriages stick and she desperately wanted their marriage to stick, regardless of why it had come about. He was her husband and she loved him so she should be able to respond to the sexual pleasure he was so good at giving.

Behind her the door to the *en suite* bathroom opened. She didn't turn around or stop brushing. The mirror in front of her reflected the sheer physical beauty of the naked man who emerged from the bathroom—a man any woman would be delighted to mate with—although the dark predatory look he shot at Tess instantly paralysed her lungs and sent a weird flutter of fear through her heart.

She'd thought she knew Nick.

But did she really?

Had he used sex to blind her to questions she should have asked before marrying him? But there was still Zack to consider. For their son's sake...

Although maybe her father was right and it was wrong to marry for the sake of a child. Wrong for her. Terribly, terribly wrong for her!

Her stomach contracted in waves of panic as Nick crossed the room to where she sat. Her chest felt as though it had steel bands around it, tightening with each step he took. She forgot to keep brushing her hair. Her mind spun with the torturous conflict of wanting this man, yet hating not being wanted for herself.

It was impossible to pretend nothing had changed.

It had changed where it counted most with Tess.

Nick was using her for financial gain.

He'd married her for financial gain.

There might be a million other reasons, as well, and all of them valid and meaningful, but Tess could not bring herself to ignore that one.

'Let me,' he said, taking the hairbrush from her motionless hand, a sensual little smile curving his sexy mouth, desire simmering in his eyes.

Let him, she told herself, hanging onto the safety of silence because maybe she could respond to his strong sexuality and be swept along by the flow of it. If she could just lose this wretched mental misery in physical sensation, drown it out...

'I swear you have the most erotic hair I've ever seen or touched,' Nick murmured, wielding the brush gently and following its bristles with his fingers.

Tess closed her eyes. Could she believe him? How much of what he said to her was true?

'And it looks best against your beautiful, bare skin,' he whispered, softly blowing the words into her ear while starting to slide the silk negligee from her shoulders.

There was no conscious decision to move. The reaction exploded from her so fast, Tess found herself on her feet, her whole body quivering as she wheeled to rebuff any further touch by Nick, the stool she'd been sitting on now standing between them, the back of her thighs pressed hard against the dressing-table, her hands clutching the edges of her robe throat-high, her eyes flaring fierce rejection.

Nick straightened up, emanating a flood of full male aggression that was not about to be turned away by anything. The muscles in his chest and arms became more sharply delineated with the tension of battle readiness. His face took on the ruthless cut of a warrior primed to beat any opposition and his eyes glittered with the determination to tear down anything that stood in the way of where he wanted to be.

'Spit it out, Tess!' he commanded, as though he'd

sensed the build-up of the emotional mountain that was now separating them.

'November the fifteenth,' burst off her tongue.

'What about it?' was whipped back at her.

'That was the day you called me, wanting to set up a meeting. You said you'd been waiting for me to get back from LA. You said you'd missed me.'

'I did miss you but I didn't say I'd been waiting for you to get back from LA,' he sharply corrected. 'I said Livvy was in Sydney so it seemed logical to expect you to be home, as well.'

It jolted the swirling chaos in her mind into a sober reassessment. Nick's recollection was more accurate than hers. He hadn't lied to her. But he hadn't told her the truth, either!

'That was the day you decided to marry me, wasn't it?' she hurled at him.

'The day I started considering a marriage with you,' he admitted, not the least bit perturbed by the accusation. 'No decision was made at that point.'

'But what made you consider it, Nick? What got your mind thinking along lines it had never travelled before?' she mocked savagely. 'What was behind that call to me on November the fifteenth?'

She saw it in his eyes—the recognition of what she now knew—but he didn't come straight out with it. He challenged for her information instead.

'Why don't you tell me, Tess?'

The silky invitation in his voice did not ring any warning bells in her raging mind. She saw it as another evasion, whipping her into laying out the truth in irrefutable terms.

'That was the day your mother received a fabulous emerald necklace from your father, Enrique Ramirez,' she punched out. 'The day you received a packet from Brazil, informing you of your father's death and laying down conditions for...'

'Naming *you* as the woman I had to marry in order to gain an inheritance?' Nick cut in, fury sparking into his eyes, lashing from his voice. 'Did my mother go as far as that, Tess?'

Not quite.

Not quite but...the implication had been there because it neatly tied up loose ends in their family history.

Yet the violent turbulence emanating from Nick checked the fierce run of her own. She was no longer so sure of where he was coming from and belatedly her memory was murmuring that Nadia Condor came from a different place. In fact, there was only one safe place to be and she offered it to the man she still wanted to keep as her husband no matter how much grief he gave her.

'Tell me the truth, Nick.'

CHAPTER TWELVE

THE truth...

The words rocketed around Nick's brain, pounding out thoughts and feelings that hadn't formed any insightful pattern because there'd been no need to stand back and define where he was at with Tess. He'd been living with her on a deeply intimate basis—time blurred by how good it was. She was his wife, the mother of his son. They were a family.

'This is the truth,' he insisted, reaching out, grabbing her hand, holding it tight, moving to pull her with him, striding for the bed. She couldn't deny how they were in bed together.

'Nick...'

The anguish in her voice goaded him into more volatile action. He swung and scooped her off her feet, cradling her tightly across his chest, his eyes stabbing through the frantic fear in hers. 'This is the truth,' he declared passionately, knowing Tess had nothing to fear from him. Absolutely nothing!

He laid her on the spill of gold and brown satin cushions, imprisoning her legs with his, the need to hold onto her urging him to cover her every possible move. His hands captured hers, stilling their wild flutter. He poured his whole life-force into crushing the doubts feeding her fear, his eyes meeting and holding hers with relentless intensity.

'What you feel with me and what I feel with you...the owning...the deep sense of union...has it ever happened for you with anyone else, Tess?' he demanded.

She remained defiantly silent, not prepared to surrender her soul to him. Fiery Tess. Icy Tess. Fighting him because of his mother's bloody-minded interference.

'No,' he answered. 'Not for you and not for me because it can only happen if the feelings are mutual, tapping into something so powerful it has to be unique to us.'

He paused, gathering himself to deliver more truth.

She was listening. She wasn't straining against his hold. He could feel the whole focus of her being gathering its concentration on what he was saying, poised to sift every word for the worth of its meaning.

'The truth is…you let my mother come into our home and destroy your trust in what we have together. My mother, who wouldn't know truth if it hit her in the face!'

'She might not know the truth but she hit me in the face with that date, Nick,' came the fierce retaliation.

'I did not marry you for money,' he retorted just as fiercely.

'No. You married me because I was probably the one woman you could think of who wouldn't bother trying to get a slice of the fabulous Ramirez estate. The woman who already had so much money to burn…'

'Stop it! Stop this absurd belittling of yourself! I won't have it! You're my wife because you're the only woman I could envisage spending my life with. Having a child with. It has nothing to do with money!'

'November the fifteenth!' she hurled at him, her

eyes flaring frustration with his refusal to attach any importance to that date.

'Was the day I decided I would not live my life as my father had,' he thundered back at her. 'He disowned me in life and by God, I disown him in death! I am *me*, the man you married, Tess. Not my mother, grasping for all she can get. Not my father who took his pleasure without caring about the lives he left in his wake. I care about you and I care about our son and our marriage is not about money. If you can't feel that…'

His eyes blazed into hers, intent on forcefully imprinting his truth. 'You *must* feel it…'

Tess lay very still, absorbing the passion pumping from Nick, deeply moved by it yet wretchedly unsure how much of his caring was actually aimed at *her*. When his mouth crashed down onto hers, ruthlessly bent on making her *feel* it, she didn't resist its wild marauding, letting her lips respond to every pressure he subjected them to, moving her tongue to the driving command of his, mentally registering every erotic sensation he incited and feeling the familiar bursts of desire building deep inside her body.

Just go with them, she told herself.

Nick might well have chosen to marry her to prove something about himself. If it wasn't for money, she could live with being the wife of his choice. As the situation stood—according to Nick—she and Zack were the beneficiaries of his personal mission to become *a family man* instead of a philanderer.

She wanted him to keep being *the family man*, and that meant keeping the sex good and giving it freely because he'd told her right at the beginning that was the glue which would make their marriage stick, and there was to be no stirring up desire without delivering, no bartering sex for other things. She had agreed and still did agree because she wanted a *have and hold* marriage with him.

'Say you feel it, Tess!' he demanded, heaving himself up to check the response in her eyes.

'Yes,' she said, because he couldn't look so fiercely determined unless the caring was there to drive such depth of feeling.

Their marriage *was* important to him. Besides, she reasoned it certainly wasn't the promise of an inheritance inspiring his love for Zack. The caring for their son was very, very real. And Tess did feel the caring for her in his next kiss.

It was much, much softer, tender, more wooing a response than compelling it. His grip on her hands loosened, the need to hold her captive to his will sliding into the desire for the mutual coming together that gave them both so much pleasure. There was no doubting the deep physical communion they invariably shared, which Nick had invoked in his argument and which Tess felt every time they made love.

Wanting to give herself up to it, wanting to forget Nadia Condor and the mercenary motives she had made so believable, wanting to make the date of November the fifteenth totally meaningless, Tess dragged her hands out from under Nick's, wound her arms around his neck and kissed him back with all the deep yearning for love in her heart.

'This is the truth,' he murmured against her lips. 'Taste it, Tess.'

'Yes,' she said.

It tasted good.

'Feel it!' he repeated, trailing slow-burn kisses down her throat, building the heat that would end up fusing them together.

It felt good.

Her fingers slithered into his hair as he shifted lower and she hugged his head to her breasts as he kissed them, making her feel voluptuously sexy, beautifully female and intensely desirable. The woman he chose as his wife, she thought. For this, not for money. She had to believe it. She did believe it.

He moved himself further down, caressing and kissing her stomach, her navel, exciting tremulous rivulets of pleasure, his tongue sliding erotically over the scar from the Caesarean operation...no, sliding reverently...projecting how much he valued the gift of his son. Their son. And for this he had married her, as well. Not for money.

She felt his truth with every sense she possessed as his mouth closed over her clitoris, driving waves of desperate delight through her body, her limbs, her every muscle. The intensity of feeling pummelled her heart. She groaned, cried out, her fingers clenching in his hair, tugging, needing, and he lifted himself to answer her need, answer it as only he ever had, giving himself into her possession, wildly, wholly, every plunge a promise of exquisite fulfilment to come.

And it ended as it always did with him possessing her, holding her to a fantastic pinnacle of pleasure as she melted around him, then fiercely concentrating on his own climax while Tess revelled in feeling his entire body straining to join his life-force with hers, exulted in feeling the tumultuous joy of it when it happened.

And, of course, this could have nothing to do with

money! It had a truth all its own...impossible to buy, impossible to simulate, impossible to deny. It was a truth that kept her warmly content within Nick's embrace afterwards, her head resting on his shoulder, her arm flung across his chest, her legs sprawled over his.

She didn't want to move.

She was with her husband, her lover, and in the secret fantasy she still nursed in her heart, her soulmate.

Nick didn't want to talk. His body was relaxed. Tess's silky hair was spread carelessly over his shoulder. Her warm breath caressed his skin. The sense of physical harmony between them did not invite any thought of conflict, yet he could not quite rid his mind of the distress his mother had inflicted on Tess.

The date—November the fifteenth—had been significant, and there *was* a link between the packet from Brazil and his decision to pursue the idea of a marriage with Tess. His denial that the link was to an inheritance from the Ramirez estate was absolutely true because nothing would ever persuade him to accept any part of his father's property. It would always feel like thirty pieces of silver to him—blood money.

But he hadn't been entirely honest with Tess. Remembering how he'd been thinking that day...it hadn't been the need to prove Enrique's opinion of him wrong that had swayed him into picking up his father's challenge. At that point in time he had arrogantly dismissed the view that his life was following the same pattern as his father's. There wasn't anything *to correct*. What had influenced his decisions and actions was the promise of a meeting with the two half-brothers he hadn't known about.

His only blood-related family.

Except that wasn't true any more. It hadn't been true from the moment Tess had told him about Zack and blown him onto a different path again. Immediate fatherhood. And fatherhood took precedence over brotherhood any day. He was living the reality of his own family right now with Tess and their son and it was so good, Nick knew he'd do everything within his power to protect it from any damage.

The weird irony was he'd barely given a thought to Enrique's challenge since Tess had presented him with Zack, yet two months down the track, Nick was beginning to feel the Brazilian playboy he'd so bitterly scorned, had finally seen the light on what was the good life. He'd written in his letter—*Find a woman you'd be happy to spend your life with, a woman you'd be happy to have children with…*

A father's advice.

Nick had mentally mocked it.

Yet he wondered now if the letter—the challenge— might not have been motivated by genuine caring…the regrets of a lifetime piling up to produce a perception Enrique had wanted to pass on to a son, a last act meant to do good at the end, hopefully redressing the harm.

Tess heaved a sigh.

Nick's arm instantly cuddled her closer to him. He dropped a kiss on the top of her head. 'Are you okay with me now, Tess?' he asked, hoping there was no poison left from his mother's visit.

'Mmmh…' It sounded like a happy hum.

'Feeling good?' He smiled confidently.

'Good sex,' she said on another sigh.

His smile faltered and died. Yet there was nothing

wrong with the comment. The sex had been good. It was always good with Tess. He had just more or less defined their relationship as great because it was never anything but good.

So why did he feel dissatisfied, frustrated, gutted because she thought that what he'd put out tonight was only *good sex*? He found himself savagely wishing she'd said something else.

But what?

What more did he want from her?

He was being unreasonable. He'd achieved what he'd set out to achieve. Tess had forgotten about his mother's rotten suppositions and they'd ended the day on a good note.

Together.

As they should be.

CHAPTER THIRTEEN

TESS was in the dining-room, watching the apple-green silk curtains being put up, feeling a warm, tingly excitement in her choice. This house was slowly turning into their home—not a showcase of intimidating possessions but a place which would soon become pleasing and harmonious and comfortable.

She was not expecting any visitors. It was Saturday morning, not a time for people to call, especially not without an appointment. It surprised her when their newly acquired housekeeper, Betty Parker, came into the dining-room to hand her a business card and announce, 'I've put the gentleman in the sitting-room, Mrs Ramirez.'

The gentleman. The rather old-fashioned term and the respectful tone in the housekeeper's voice instantly piqued Tess's curiosity. The extremely efficient Betty Parker was only in her late forties with a very modern outlook on life. Clearly she was highly impressed by the visitor.

Tess glanced at the card for identification. Shock punched her heart and chilled her skin.

Javier Estes…an attorney…a Rio de Janeiro address.

There could be only one connection—the Ramirez estate in Brazil. And why would a lawyer fly all the way to Sydney if there wasn't an inheritance to administer?

It had to be about money.

And if there was money…Nick had lied to her!

'Mr Estes asked to see Mr Ramirez,' Betty informed her, 'but since he's down at the pool terrace with the baby…'

Teaching Zack to swim in the heated spa pool and Zack was taking to the water like a little tadpole…their son…with his father…who loved him. Did it matter so much that Nick didn't love her? That he'd married her for…

For what?

Tess's teeth clenched.

She didn't know yet but she was going to find out!

'You were right to come and tell me before fetching Nick, Betty,' she quickly assured the housekeeper, handing back the card. 'Take this down to him now while I go and greet Mr Estes and keep him company.'

Betty smiled and nodded, confiding, 'I thought he had to be a very important gentleman, not to be kept waiting too long, and with Mr Ramirez in the pool…'

'Absolutely right. Thank you.'

It would be fifteen minutes, at least, before Nick could appear respectably dressed, as he'd undoubtedly want to be for this visitor. Tess had no qualms whatsoever about greeting the Brazilian as she was, her fawn slacks and the striped shirt in fawn, sky-blue and white, being definitely in the class of smart casual at home.

The sitting-room was one of the few rooms Tess had finished furnishing to her satisfaction. Amazingly she had picked up all the pieces at auction and she loved how right the arrangement looked to her eyes; the three chesterfields upholstered in shades of cream and peach and a very pastel apple-green, the marble coffee tables with their subtle swirls of peach, the

complementary pattern in the main floor rug...but the
lawyer from Brazil was not admiring any of this. He
was not seated, either. He stood by the full-length windows, gazing out at the view of Sydney Harbour.

'Mr Estes...'

He swung around and Tess had an instant appreciation of the impact he'd had on the housekeeper. He
was tall and the fine head of perfectly groomed white
hair framing the dark olive-skinned patrician face gave
him a look of commanding authority. His shoulders
did not have the stoop of age yet Tess judged the man
to be in his seventies from the deeply carved lines in
his cheeks and the sag of what had once been a formidable jawline.

He was beautifully dressed in a grey silk suit—ac-
cessorised to sartorial perfection. He looked like big
money and he most certainly represented big money,
and if she hadn't been around big money all her life,
Tess might well have felt intimidated by Javier Estes.
As it was, the sight of him sickened her and she found
herself bristling with aggression, wanting to fight
whatever he was bringing into her home.

For several moments it appeared he stared sharply
at her, the set of faintly tinted rimless glasses he wore
making her unsure of his expression. But then his
mouth curved into a disarming smile and he spoke her
name as though he found it charming to attach it to
her.

'Tessa Steele...'

'Tessa Steele Ramirez,' she clipped out, establishing her marital status to Nick as she moved forward
to offer her hand.

'Of course.' *His* hands formed a quick, graceful gesture, appealing for sympathetic understanding. 'A cu-

riosity for me that Enrique's son chose his wife from the Steele family since there had been...shall we say...a scandalous connection?'

'That wasn't of Nick's making. Nor of mine,' she stated dismissively, relieved to hear confirmation that she had been Nick's choice..a surprising one to this man.

'Which makes you both strongly individual people,' he remarked, his gaze roving over her hair before he added admiringly, 'And you are strikingly beautiful.' He enfolded her hand in both of his, pressing lightly as his eyes definitely glinted with male appreciation, despite his age. 'I can see why many things might be overlooked, given a woman such as yourself.'

'Likewise, many things might be overlooked because Nick is the man he is, Mr Estes,' Tess dryly retorted. 'But let's move on from surface judgements and get to whatever purpose has brought you all the way from Brazil.' She extracted her hand and waved towards the sofa grouping. 'Shall we sit down?'

'I was waiting for your husband.'

'He will be here shortly. In the meantime...'

She moved to seat herself, expecting him to follow but he didn't. He remained standing by the windows, watching her settle herself. Tess had the feeling he was keenly observing everything about her, fitting answers to questions he had in his mind. It seemed to validate Nadia Condor's contention that Nick's marrying her *was* linked to an inheritance from his father, which put Tess even more on edge about Nick's lying to her about it.

'Being a lawyer and coming from Rio de Janeiro, I assume you have something to do with executing the will of Enrique Ramirez, Mr Estes,' she put forward, probing for information.

'I am the sole executor,' he conceded. Then with an air of considerable pride, he added, 'Enrique entrusted me with judging if each mission was fulfilled in spirit as well as on paper.'

'Each *mission*?' Tess quizzed, finding the term rather odd.

One eyebrow arched, challenging her ignorance. 'You are unaware of the conditions attached to your husband's inheritance from his father?'

There it was—the link to Nick's marriage proposal!

'Since I don't know of any inheritance, I can hardly be aware of conditions,' she shot back at the lawyer, her chin lifting with considerable pride of her own as she added, 'I did not marry my husband for money, Mr Estes.'

His mouth twitched in ironic amusement. 'I did not imagine it would be a factor to you, given the wealth of your own family. But there is most certainly an inheritance at stake here…'

'Like hell there is!'

The furious words cracked across the room as Nick charged into it, barely clothed in one of the white towelling robes kept in the dressing rooms at the pool. It hung loosely from his shoulders, gaping at the front because he clearly hadn't stopped long enough to drag its edges together and do up the tie-belt. The brief black swimsuit he wore underneath it was clearly visible.

Zack, probably still as naked as he'd been in the pool, was wrapped in a towel and riding in the crook of Nick's arm, his little face looking brilliantly alert to the fascination of his father in steaming attack mode, his gaze following Nick's other arm as it stabbed out at Javier Estes then swept back, pointing to the door.

'Get out of our home!'

'Nick!' The shocked gasp literally exploded from Tess's lips as she leapt to her feet, the urge to intervene driven by his appalling lack of civility.

His eyes were like green shards of ice, determined on freezing any further action from her. 'Keep out of this, Tess! This man has no business here with us. He came uninvited. He is not welcome. He goes with the same nothing Enrique Ramirez granted me when I was eighteen.'

'I came to give,' Javier Estes argued.

'I don't want what you came to give. I didn't want any part of what my father denied me while he was alive, and I certainly don't want it after he's dead. If you assumed I would take it, you could not be more wrong.'

'You fulfilled the conditions.'

'Not to benefit from the Ramirez estate,' was whipped back so fast, there was no leeway granted for argument.

'I can still award a third of it...'

'No!'

The old man gestured urgently to Zack. 'You have a son...Enrique's grandson...'

'Leave my boy out of this.'

'Why would you deny him his heritage?'

'Because the only heritage that counts is right here with his mother and me.' Nick strode over to Tess, his free arm gathering her close to him to present a united family to Javier Estes. 'Tess and I will bring up our son *our* way. To value what *we* value. And that's about loving him, caring about the person he is and always being there for him. Zack doesn't need anything from Enrique Ramirez.'

Tess stood in the secure circle of his arm, feeling the fiercely proud independence pumping from Nick and encompassing her as an essential part of what he wanted in his life. Partners, she thought in deep relief, finally dismissing the painful conflict stirred by the arrival of Javier Estes.

A partnership was what Nick had proposed in the beginning. It had nothing to do with gaining an inheritance. It was about sharing what they believed was important for children. And happily sharing a bed, as well. It wasn't *all* she wanted, but…the sick anxiety she had carried into this room was draining away.

Nick had not lied to her.

The lawyer from Brazil did not appear at all perturbed by Nick's violent and vehement outburst. He seemed to look approvingly on the family grouping which was being flaunted at him. After a few moments of silently weighing what he'd just been told, he calmly asked, 'You think Enrique didn't care about you?'

'I remember my meeting with him in Rio de Janeiro very well,' Nick retorted with bitter derision. 'One could say everything about it was indelibly imprinted on my brain.'

'As it was on Enrique's,' came the soberly paced reply. 'Why do you imagine he paid to get reports on your life for the past sixteen years?'

Reports? Did Nick know he'd been under surveillance? It made Tess feel creepy even thinking about it, but Nick did not seem surprised by the claim. He glared at Javier Estes in grim-faced silence as the law-yer put forward another argument.

'Why do you imagine he constructed the letter he did for you before he died—the task he set you in the hope of changing what he knew to be a life of hollow pleasures...' His gaze moved, pointedly encompassing Zack and Tess before adding, '...into what you have now?'

Tess's mind instantly seized on *the letter*.

Received on November the fifteenth with the packet from Brazil?

Was getting married and starting a family part of the task—the mission he had to carry out before...but why do it when he didn't want the inheritance? Why rush into proposing to her if there was no other agenda on the line? It made no sense.

Nick's arm around her tightened as he growled, 'What I have now is due to Tess—the person she is and what *she* has given me.'

She silently savoured those words. They weren't hollow. They were loaded with meaning, making her feel truly important to Nick.

The old man nodded and smiled. 'I can see that your commitment to each other is genuine. Enrique would be pleased.'

Nick's hand knifed the air in disgust. 'I did not marry Tess to please my father.'

An eyebrow arched in challenge. 'Can you deny that his letter prompted you into thinking about mar-riage? There is...considerable serendipity...in the tim-ing.'

There certainly is, Tess thought.

As Nadia Condor had observed to extremely hurtful effect.

'Serendipity, yes,' Nick bitingly conceded, 'but my marriage to Tess still has nothing to do with the conditions Enrique laid down for inheriting whatever he'd decided was my share of his estate.'

'The inheritance…' The lawyer flip-flopped his hand, indicating that it was an ambivalent factor. 'Enrique simply used it as a power tool to drive you into reappraising your life. It worked, did it not?'

Breath hissed out from between Nick's clenched teeth. He was steaming over this manipulation from the grave, yet Tess reasoned it had done him no harm. Even if it was rebellion against his father's appraisal of his life that had spurred him into proposing marriage to her, it had led to what they shared now. And Nick certainly valued it enough to come charging in to protect it.

'You actually sowed the seeds of caring by confronting Enrique when you were eighteen,' the lawyer went on. 'He could not acknowledge your existence without destroying the powerful connections that had become the fabric of his life, but his wife had not borne him sons—only two sickly daughters—and she could not give him any more children. It hurt him to turn you away.'

'Tough!' Nick mocked. 'Forgive me but I'm not impressed with my value rising because my father couldn't have legitimate sons.'

'It was coming face to face with you that made him care,' the lawyer shot back, his long elegant hands making a comprehensive gesture at Nick as he explained further. 'The boy—the young man—you were at eighteen. You made him want to know you. As the years went on and his wife died of leukaemia and both daughters passed away from other ailments, Enrique became more and more obsessed with your life.'

'I'm not impressed with having my life spied upon, either,' Nick said in savage rejection of his father's obsession. 'If that's still happening, call off the watch-dogs, Estes, because…'

'He also watched over the lives of your two half-brothers whom he searched out after he'd sent you away.'

Half-brothers?

Tess's mind boggled over the shockingly broadened picture the lawyer had just drawn.

Words exploded from Nick, seemingly shot from an eruption of jealous fury. 'He met *them*? Acknowl-edged *them* as his sons?'

The deep poison of rejection was spilling out.

'No.' Javier Estes shook his head with a rueful air. 'The structure of their lives was such that Enrique judged it wiser for him to remain unknown.'

'Oh, come on!' Nick tersely challenged, his disbe-lief in any sensitivity from his father pouring into scorn. 'They would have interfered with his life, just as I would have. Much safer to leave any contact until after he was dead.'

'Perhaps that is true. But he cared enough about all three of you to give you to each other…*if* that was what you wanted.'

'Give? A gift comes free, Estes. A gift is not at-tached to conditions.'

'Each mission was designed for the good of each son.'

'*Each* mission?' Nick's voice climbed with outrage. '*Each…mission?*'

Zack decided he should match his father's outburst

with a full-blooded scream. Even a four-month-old baby was not immune to the tensions running riot in this room, Tess thought, taking him in her arms as Nick thrust him at her in distracted agitation, beyond the task of soothing their son when all his own testosterone was fired up to blast the executor of Enrique Ramirez's will right back to the world he came from—a world Nick clearly rejected with every atom of his being.

'Best take Zack out of here, Tess,' he muttered, his eyes flickering with barely controllable fury.

'No.' She quickly tucked Zack's head into the curve of her neck and shoulder—his favourite comforter place—bringing down the volume of his distress to a snuffling whimper as she rubbed her cheek over the soft springy curls on his head. 'Whatever's going on here we stand together,' she insisted, her own eyes flashing unshakable determination.

No way was she going to miss out on information which would answer so much about how Nick thought and felt!

He sucked in a deep breath, his chest expanding to muscle-bristling tension as he faced the lawyer again. In a dangerously low voice throbbing with all manner of threats, he posed the question, 'Are you telling me that any meeting with my half-brothers is conditional upon *their* performing missions set by *our father* before he died?'

'That is correct, yes.'

'There never was any guarantee of a meeting with them even if I did *my part* in fulfilling my father's fantasy?'

'You each had to earn the right to...'

'The right!' Nick completely lost it. 'Don't you see

how obscene this is? How absolutely, grotesquely obscene? We're not his sons. We're his performing monkeys!'

He threw out his hands in furious disgust as he advanced on Javier Estes. 'And you...you're the director of his circus. Having fun, are you? Seeing how well the outcast bastards are coming into Enrique's fold and toeing his line, handing out rewards to them for being good little monkeys...'

Javier Estes stiffened in the face of oncoming attack. 'I assure you, sir, it was not meant to be like that. There were lifestyle issues...'

'They're my brothers!' Nick shouted him down. 'They belong to me by blood! Let them reject me as they might, but Enrique did not have the right to give out knowledge of our existence, then keep us apart. We're men with the right to choose for ourselves.'

'Do you not think your brotherhood would naturally become more meaningful if you each had a mission to complete in order to meet at all?' Estes argued earnestly.

'Twist it any way you like...' Nick hurled at him from a bare metre away, then forced himself to come to a halt, his hands clenched, his chin jutting aggressively as he emphatically declared, '...it is still an obscene misuse of power and I will not be party to it. Not to any of it. I do not *need* what Enrique could have given me. I now have my own family.'

He backed off, raising a warning hand to the lawyer who was opening his mouth to speak again. 'Enough! Call off the watchdogs. Go back to Brazil. We have no business together. It's over. Finished.' His hands scissored the air with violent decisiveness. 'Gone!'

Nick turned his back on Javier Estes and strode

straight over to Tess, plucked Zack out of her hold and nestled their son against his shoulder. 'I'm taking him back to the swimming pool, Tess. If you want to see this guy out, do so. Or get Betty to do it. I'm all out of being polite to circus directors.'

Tess nodded, acutely aware of major turbulence driving him. She was vividly reminded of when she'd told him her father had sat with her during Zack's birth. Nick's sense of rightness had been hugely, deeply violated. It was again now.

Blood ties...his son's birth being kept from him...his brothers being kept from him...

She watched him carry their child out of the room. Their departure was followed by a silence loaded with far too much painful family history to be easily bridged. Javier Estes did not move to take his leave, didn't even suggest it. He seemed rooted to the spot, perhaps shocked into a reassessment of his role as executor of a will that viewed people as puppets to be manipulated into play.

'This is a sad business,' he finally murmured, grimacing over his failure to win Nick's co-operation with the master plan.

'A gift might have been good, Mr Estes,' Tess said quietly. 'Something freely given...'

'When has something freely given ever been valued?' he tossed at her derisively, then shook his head. 'It seemed he was complying with the conditions...'

'What were the conditions?' Tess asked, determined on knowing the full truth now.

'To find a woman he loved, marry her, have a child, set up a family life...stop flitting aimlessly from woman to woman in empty relationships.' The lawyer gestured an appeal. 'Is that not good advice? Does it not suggest a father's caring to you?'

A woman he loved...

The watchdogs had apparently missed the point that she'd already had Nick's child and their marriage was based on love for their son, not love for each other.

'I came because he had not contacted me,' the lawyer said in frustration. 'The other two had. It was the natural thing to do.'

'The other brothers?'

'Yes. And the meeting date has been set.'

'They have completed their missions?'

He frowned. 'I'm not at liberty to say.'

'But the meeting date has been set,' Tess pressed, thinking how pointless it was to set a date if no one was going to turn up.

'February the fourteenth. Four o'clock in the afternoon. In my office,' he reeled off.

'In Rio de Janeiro?'

'Of course. There is the matter of settling the estate.'

'Nick is not about to change his mind on the inheritance, Mr Estes,' Tess said, mocking that purpose.

He winced. 'The face to face rejection when he was eighteen...it is not forgotten, nor forgiven. It is a rather bleak irony, do you not think, that it was he who impressed Enrique so much...' He sighed. '...and he who gains nothing from it?'

'Perhaps the other brothers did not have such a *displaced* life. For Nick and for me...having to pay a price for what should be our natural rights as human beings...it eats at our souls, Mr Estes. And we have to save ourselves from that, or at least limit the damage.'

A musing little smile curled his lips and his eyes seemed to glint with respectful admiration. 'You understand him.'

'I love him,' she stated simply.

A slow nod of acknowledgement. 'I regret that I cannot break the terms of the will. I cannot *give* him his brothers. If you love him, Tessa Steele Ramirez, you will not leave him displaced. You know the date and time for the meeting...'

But I didn't say Nick loved me back, Mr Estes.

She escorted the lawyer from Brazil to the front door, watched him leave, then wandered back through the beautiful family home Nick had bought for them, reviewing in her mind every step made to where they were now.

Their marriage had nothing to do with an inheritance. Nadia Condor had been very wrong about that. But had Nick started on this journey with her to get to his brothers?

Had the destination of the journey changed?

If so...when and why?

Tess kept seeing the image of a set of scales being loaded with her and Zack on one side and Nick's two half-brothers on the other. The weight had been dramatically tipped this morning with the brothers being discarded. Nevertheless, this did not leave Tess with any sense of winning. She knew Nick was losing and there was no way of forgetting the pain of his loss.

It had to be addressed.

CHAPTER FOURTEEN

NICK felt too raw, too angry, too *exposed*, to be anywhere near Tess. Nor was he in a fit frame of mind to
be looking after their son. It was wrong to use his own
fatherhood as a blind to the churning hatred stirred by
his father's attitude towards himself and his brothers—
owing them nothing except their lives, giving them
nothing, not even each other. He had to deal with this
alone, get past it, move on into his future.

He sought out Carol Tunny, the Karitane nurse who
was now an integral part of their household, finding
her in the nursery quarters where Zack was due to
have his morning nap. Having left his son in her care,
he decided what he needed was some hard, mindless,
physical task to get rid of this sickening inner turbulence.

He headed for the boatshed beside the wharf, dis-
carding the white bathrobe at the pool terrace on his
way down to the harbour foreshore. His small racing
yacht was up on the slips, ready for the hull to be
scraped clean of barnacles—precisely the kind of job
that should work him back in control of himself.

He'd been at it for a good hour when Tess walked
in. He stopped scraping and stared at her, realising she
probably had some issues rising out of the Brazilian
lawyer's visit, though he'd gone all out to refute the
inheritance shadow on their marriage. She couldn't believe that any more.

Yet he sensed the barriers were up again.

She looked as cool, calm and collected as she'd always been when they'd worked together, discussing the casting of the right people for particular projects. Her clothes were neatly co-ordinated, smart but not sexy, her make-up minimal, her glorious red-gold hair pulled back into a pony-tail because of the summer heat, although quite a few provocative little ringlets escaped confinement.

To Nick's intense chagrin, it wasn't just her appearance reminding him of former times. It was the *on guard* expression on her face, the wariness sharpening the clear blue of her lovely eyes. The intimacy of their marriage should have changed this. The violent feelings he'd been working hard at setting aside, boiled up into frustration that Tess still didn't trust him.

'Hot work,' she remarked, shooting a glance over his sweaty, grime-streaked chest and arms. Her gaze didn't fall as low as the brief swimming costume he was still wearing. In fact, it quickly diverted to the small bar-fridge in the corner of the boatshed. 'Can I get you a cold drink, Nick?' she asked, already moving to supply it.

She was nervous of him.

He hated that, too.

'Yes. Thanks,' he said, trying to sound civilised, conscious that he probably looked as though he'd walked out of a primitive jungle. He strode over to the sink to wash up. 'I take it you've sent Javier Estes packing.'

'He's gone,' she stated simply.

'And you want to talk about it,' he slung at her as he turned on the taps.

'Yes.' She opened the door of the small refrigerator and studied what was stocked on its shelves.

At least she was being direct this time, Nick told himself, not silently bottling up her concerns as she had after the visit of his mother. He grabbed the soap and a washing sponge, splashed water over his face, arms and chest, then worked at presenting a cleaner, cooler aspect of himself. He was towelling himself dry as Tess placed a cold can of flavoured mineral water on the sink. He reached out to grab her wrist, to hold her beside him.

'I never wanted the inheritance, Tess,' he stated, his eyes blazing into hers, fiercely intent on burning that fact into her brain so it couldn't ever be in dispute again.

Her gaze dropped to the strong encirclement of his hand. 'But you did have another agenda, Nick,' she said quietly. 'When you proposed marriage to me, you were thinking of getting to your brothers.'

'Was I?'

It forced her gaze to lift again, to meet his in challenge. He challenged right back.

'Maybe I used the idea of them as an excuse to go after what I really wanted with you, Tess.'

She frowned, then gave him an aching look that begged the truth, no fancy side-steps, no dressing up what had moved him to change the status quo of their *work only* relationship. 'November the fifteenth,' she reminded him.

The truth…

Strange how hard it was to surrender it, even to instil the trust which he knew was vital to the life he now had. But there was no alternative, no diversionary tactic that would leave him less exposed to her, no shield to hide the poverty which had plagued his life, despite all the material riches that had been there for the taking. Only the truth would serve what he most needed in their relationship.

Nick set down the towel and drew Tess into a loose embrace as he focused his mind on seeking the best path towards understanding. He rested his forehead lightly on hers, needing their minds to meet. 'You have a family,' he started. 'It may be dysfunctional but you've met every member of it. You know what they're like, you know where they come from, and you can mix freely with them, both on your mother's side and your father's.'

Her shoulders pulled back, muscles tensing, whether in impatience or resistance he couldn't tell, but she was not in tune with this talk about her family.

'That's not to say you weren't alone, Tess, and were very lonely most of the time,' he pushed on. 'I know this.'

A soft sigh whispered from her lips, relaxing the stiffness, but she said nothing, waiting for more from him.

'The packet from Brazil…learning I have two half-brothers, illegitimate sons like me, one in the USA and one in Britain…and being told I don't get to meet them or even know who they are unless the lawyer handling the Ramirez estate is convinced I've met my father's challenge…suddenly *I* had a family, Tess. I wasn't alone. There were two other guys out there connected to me by blood.'

'I do realise that had to be important to you, Nick,' she murmured.

A derisive little laugh gravelled from his throat. 'I felt like a long distance runner who'd been forced to run his race alone, not knowing he had brothers running parallel to himself. It made me think...that bastard who was our father kept them from me while he was alive, but be damned if I was going to let him keep them from me in death!'

'Nor should you.' She tipped her head back to look directly at him. 'That's what I came down here to say.'

'No, Tess. I don't want Enrique Ramirez living on in me. I don't want to see him living on in my brothers, still pulling our strings. Nor do I want the shadow of his influence on any part of our life together.'

'But...'

He quickly placed a silencing finger on her lips, hating the painful protest in her eyes. 'No. Listen to me.' He cupped her face, softly caressing the anxiety lines from the corners of her eyes, feeling an urgent tenderness that had to be expressed. 'You think I began this journey with you because of the packet from Brazil. And yes, it was the trigger that got me moving, but even as I read my father's challenge, I thought...Tess. As I stoked the desire to meet my brothers, I thought...Tess. There was never the slightest question in my mind as to whom I might ask to marry me.'

'You gave me many logical reasons,' she reminded him.

'Being reasonable was more acceptable to my long-held cynical view of life, love and marriage, but there was no reason whatsoever in the powerful feelings you stirred in me, Tess, and you must know reason flew completely out the door once you told me about Zack.'

She looked at him wonderingly, not quite convinced by what he was telling her.

'Surely you understand everything changed that

night when I was confronted by you—already the mother of my child—and our son. It gave me the most intimate connections I could have, and I'm not like my father, Tess. I will not walk away. I will *never* walk away from what we have together and what we can give our children together.'

Tess felt the pain behind Nick's outpouring, the emptiness of a life that had known far more about rejection than connection. The realisation hit her that the one connection he had lived with—his mother—had never inspired trust in him. The reverse, in fact. Which explained much of how he had dealt with women.

He didn't trust.

Yet to fulfil his father's challenge he'd had to trust one woman enough to have a child by her—a woman who wouldn't cheat him of what was his. He'd chosen her without a moment's thought to any of the other women who'd streamed through his life. An intuitive choice or not, it was undoubtedly the biggest compliment he could ever give a woman and he'd given it to her.

She'd been standing in the circle of his embrace with her hands curled into fists against his chest, intent on holding off the sexual magnetism he could use to deflect her purpose in coming down here. It was impossible now to stop her fingers from uncurling, spreading across the vital strength of the man, over his heart, her own heart swelling with love for him—for the boy who'd been as lonely as she had been, more so since she had never been cruelly rejected by her father—for the man who'd broken his proudly guarded isolation to take *her* hand in a marriage aimed at making his own family.

'Thank you for trusting me, Nick,' she said softly, her fingers stroking the taut muscles supporting the pride which would still have him stand alone if he had to. 'Thank you for explaining the truth of how it was. It matters a lot to me.'

She knew intuitively he would retreat from her if she didn't show her belief in him. Now was the moment to capture an intimacy they hadn't reached before. 'I'm sorry I listened to your mother. She conjured up things that have plagued my life and although I tried to look past them, I needed you to set them aside for me, to make me feel right with you again.'

'Have I done that?' he asked with urgent intensity.

'Yes,' she answered emphatically. 'Yes, you have.'

A fierce triumph blazed from his eyes. 'Good! Because *you* are right for me, Tess. So very right in every way there is.'

It would be easy now just to revel in the rightness he felt with her, to hold him to herself and let no one else into their private little world, but Tess knew she would never feel right with herself if she did that. Love was about giving, not taking. Nick wanted his brothers. He might well have come to her and Zack eventually, but the thought of his brothers had brought him much sooner, giving Zack his father, giving her her husband...*until death*.

Nick had meant the vows.

There would be no walking away.

Ever.

She totally believed that now.

She took a deep breath and lifted a hand to his face, her eyes begging a stay in judgement. 'Do you think it's right to shut out your brothers when they've done whatever your father demanded of them in order to meet you, Nick? All these months, wanting a connection with you...'

'More likely wanting the inheritance,' he cut in with harsh cynicism.

'What if they're like you and don't care about the inheritance?' she swiftly argued. 'What if they've made their own way in life and been just as successful as you in their chosen careers, yet they've always felt alone and disconnected with the rest of the human race?'

He grimaced over her description, his eyes flashing a savage irony as he said, 'They may not be like me at all, Tess. I may have absolutely nothing in common with them.'

'But you do, Nick. You share a father who didn't care enough to make himself known to you in life, but who challenged the caring in all three of his sons after he died. It seems to me he was saying to each one of you...how much caring do you have in your hearts?'

'More than *he* ever had.'

'But you're letting that lack in him block your path to your brothers, Nick, and you'll be on the losing end again if you do that. This is your chance to break free of the blight your father cast over your life. It's the way to move past it.'

He frowned as though he wasn't grasping the logic of her argument, or grasping its significance all too strongly.

'You have a choice here,' Tess plunged on. 'You can hold out your hand to your brothers or turn your back on them. If you turn your back, Nick, if you reject the chance of meeting them and getting to know them...' She lifted her other hand to cup his face and

plead earnestly with the heart and soul behind his eyes.
'...*you will be just like your father.*'

'No!' His head jerked out of her hold in emphatic
negation. He stepped back, his hands moving to close
around her upper arms, maybe wanting to shake her
out of a contention which was so violently offensive
to him.

'Yes!' she pressed, reckless in her determination to
resolve this issue. 'It's what he did to you. What he
did to them. And they're going to Rio de Janeiro to
meet you. Your blood brothers, Nick. The other two
outcast illegitimate sons. They'll be there in Javier
Estes' office at four o'clock in the afternoon of
February the fourteenth...'

'How do you know this?

'I asked.'

'Why?' His fingers dug into the soft flesh below her
shoulders. 'Why would you care whether I meet them
or not?'

'Because *you* care...' She took a deep breath, and
riding the wave of wildly heightened emotion that
swirled from him, gave up her most secret truth.
'...and I love you.' Her mouth twisted into a wry little
smile at her own helplessly stated confession. 'Quite
simply, Nick, I want the best for you.'

'You love me.' He repeated the words as though he
was amazed by them. The pressure of his fingers on
her arms eased. His eyes searched hers with an incredulous expression that moved slowly into a won-
drous joy, spilling into a smile that caused her heart
to pitter-patter all around her chest. 'You love me,' he
intoned again, obviously relishing the sound of it and
the sense of it.

'Don't start thinking you can take advantage of

that,' she warned, reacting to a spurt of panic. 'I've got a highly developed sense of what's fair, Nick Ramirez.'

'And fair's fair,' he agreed. 'I'd like to have that absolutely established before I admit I love you, my beautiful Tess.'

It sucked the air right out of her lungs. She had to gasp for breath just to weakly repeat, 'You love me?'

'Hmmm...' His eyes narrowed in consideration. 'Maybe a mutual enslavement can work. It's the love factor being out of balance that causes misery and mayhem.'

She slammed her hand against his chest to force his focus back onto her. 'You actually do love me?'

'To distraction,' he answered in mock exasperation. 'Terrible distraction. I suspected it would happen if I let you get really close to me and here I've been, fighting like crazy to get you to trust me, desperate to convince you that you're at the centre of the world I truly care about, ready to do anything...'

'Anything?' she inserted giddily, her mind swimming in a cocktail of happiness.

He looked edgy. 'Almost anything.'

She slid her hands up around his neck and stepped closer. His eyes glinted with suspicion and some swiftly developing wicked plans of his own. Tess thought how amazing it was that he could so quickly excite a build-up of sexual awareness, of desire for fast and flagrant physical intimacy.

'So are you going to Rio for the fourteenth of February?' she quickly slipped in.

'If you come with me,' he decided without any trouble at all.

'I'll be with you,' she promised.

He nodded. 'I've come to the conclusion that it's not sex that glues a marriage together. What really makes it stick is loving each other.'

'I do love you, Nick,' she said for the sheer joy of revelling in the freedom to say it.

'Let's see how much.'

He kissed her.

And she showed him how much, which inspired him to show her a lot more.

Even in a boatshed, the sex was good.

But it wasn't the only good thing in their marriage.

CHAPTER FIFTEEN

NICK had wanted to give this party before they left for
Rio de Janeiro, its purpose to publicly celebrate their
marriage which he still felt was important to do. Their
happiness together, he declared, would confound
everyone and make it a scintillating affair, all the
guests glittering madly around them, trying to shine
light on cracks in their relationship and forced to concede failure because there were none.

And that was certainly happening tonight, Tess
thought, secretly amused by some of the outrageous
questions tossed at both her and Nick as they stood
arm in arm, greeting and chatting to guests who were
rolling up despite the short notice. The whole A-list
of Sydney society was agog to assess the newly married couple and see what they'd done to the much
envied dress circle residence at Point Piper.

The funny part was, Tess knew that only a short
while ago she would have hated this kind of scene.
The secure knowledge that Nick loved her made a
world of difference. It simply didn't matter how they
were viewed as a couple or what anyone said to them,
the happiness in her heart could not be diminished or
soured or poisoned.

Besides, generally people did wish them well, and
even the envy seemed reasonably good-natured.
Perhaps genuine happiness was infectious. Whatever…it was easy to smile and keep on smiling, even
in the face of Nadia Condor's flaunting of the

fabulous emerald necklace—her gift from Enrique Ramirez for producing such an outstanding son. Naturally she had chosen a classic black gown to show off the jewellery.

'So you're both travelling to Rio to collect,' she said with smug confidence in *her* reading of the situation. Nadia's beautiful golden eyes shimmered with pleasure. 'I knew you'd take the inheritance.'

'Actually we're just going to meet my brothers,' Nick drawled. 'Should have a fun time. And while we're there I'll sign my share of the inheritance over to an orphanage.'

The pleasure jolted into shock. 'An orphanage?'

'Yes. Tess and I think that would be very appropriate, don't we, darling?'

'There are so many children who are alone in this world,' she inserted, adding sympathetically, 'You must remember losing everything yourself when you were sixteen, Nadia.'

Her head lifted in haughty disdain. 'I've come a long way since I was sixteen.'

A long way...but to Tess's mind, Nadia had never arrived where she and Nick were now and probably never would. Which was sad. Impulsively she said, 'I was wondering—with all your experience of decorating houses, Nadia—if I could ask your advice on a few things when Nick and I get back.'

The disdain was instantly replaced by delighted anticipation. 'My dear, I'm sure we could have a lovely girls' time together. Just call me.'

'I will,' Tess promised.

Nadia sailed off with the sublimely confident air of a queen about to inspect her domain and order improvements on it in the very near future.

'She'll try to take over,' Nick muttered in warning.

'A bit of giving won't hurt.' Tess raised an eloquently knowing gaze to his. 'She needs us in her life, Nick. We're the only family she's got.'

His mouth tilted into a wry smile as he nodded. 'Okay, but you need to know my mother always aims to get her own way. Don't hesitate to yell for help when she moves the line beyond what's acceptable.'

She grinned. 'I'll yell.'

'And remember you come first with me. You are not and never will be in competition with my mother.'

She laughed, blissfully sure of his support.

He lowered his head to whisper in her ear, 'If you keep looking at me like that, I'm going to have to race you off to bed and...'

'Can't! Here comes *my* mother.'

He gave a mock groan and resumed the role of party host.

While Nadia Condor's style was regal, expecting everyone to worship at her court, admiring her unique and outstanding beauty, Livvy Curtin's style was totally flamboyant, expecting everyone to be dazzled into courting her for her magnificent theatrical value.

Tonight she was wearing a gown in dark red and purple satin—amazing with her now strawberry-blonde hair topping it off and jet-black jewellery to provide dramatic contrast. Of course, her main accessory was the thirty-something gym-toned gorgeous hunk on her arm, and Tess had to concede her mother didn't look much older, due to the many little surgical procedures she'd had done over the years.

Of course, she was late arriving. Livvy was always late arriving anywhere. It increased her own sense of worth to have people waiting for her—the power of a

star. She descended upon Tess and Nick now as
though she was bestowing a favour on them with her
presence.

'Married! With child! And home! How very do-
mestic, darlings!' she trumpeted at them, moving into
her air-kiss routine. 'Though I must say this house
does have a brilliant setting.'

'Nice to know something meets with your approval,' Tess couldn't help drawling.

'You're always so literal, Tessa. Actually you're
looking better tonight than I've ever seen you.
Positively blooming.' She batted her long false eyelashes at Nick in flirtatious appreciation of his obvious
virility. 'You must be taking good care of my baby's
needs.'

Baby!

Tess rolled her eyes. Of course taking years off her
daughter's age took years off Livvy's own.

'Well, she's certainly taking good care of mine,'
Nick replied, his voice rich with warm satisfaction.

'Really? I always thought Tessa took more after
Brian than me—so uptight and inhibited and straight.'
She actually reached out and patted Tess's cheek. 'I'm
delighted to hear you have some of my heart and soul,
darling.'

Tess gritted her teeth in exasperation over her
mother's view on life and love. 'There's more to marriage than good sex, Mother,' she bit out.

It was the unforgiveable sin, calling Livvy Mother,
and it instantly provoked a withdrawal from family
intimacy. 'If you're going to talk in such boring plat-
itudes, Tessa...'

'I've always been boring,' Tess waved her mother

and her current toy-boy on. 'I'm sure you'll find more exciting company amongst our guests.'

'I do hope so, dear,' she huffed and sailed off to command adoring attention elsewhere.

'That was not your usual gracious self, Tess,' Nick commented, arching a quizzical eyebrow at her.

She heaved a sigh to rid herself of tension. 'Sorry! I find my mother endlessly embarrassing. I guess I am just as uptight and inhibited and straight as my father.'

'Not so I've noticed.'

'I felt she was reducing you to beefcake. Which is what she does to all men,' Tess added in rueful explanation.

'The Hollywood Dream runs on desirability,' Nick said seriously. 'You have to understand Livvy is obsessed with that and everything she does and says is probably aimed at bolstering her sense of desirability.'

'Including the toy-boy?'

'It has a currency.' He slanted her a sardonic little smile. 'It's all about counting her worth, Tess, just as my mother tots up possessions to count hers. Neither of them is about to change these ingrained habits. We just have to accept them as they are. And occasionally, we can even enjoy who they are.'

Tess thought about it, deciding it was probably fair comment. Sad comment. So okay, before the party ended she would make peace with Livvy and keep the doors open. Maybe somewhere down the line of the future, her mother might want to be a mother. And a grandmother.

Much later in the evening her father drew her aside from the discussion Nick was having with a film producer whose work he admired. 'Fine party, Tessa,' he remarked.

'I'm glad you're enjoying it, Dad.'

He gave a dry chuckle. 'A bit like the three-ring circus you reckoned a wedding would be, though for me it's been quite amusing observing the prima donnas staking out their own centre stages.' His shaggy white eyebrows lifted in query. 'No distress for you in it?'

She shook her head. 'They can't touch what Nick and I have together.'

'So it's working out fine for you.'

'As fine as it could be, Dad.'

Her father put his arm around her shoulders to give them a warm hug. 'I just wanted to tell you how proud I am of you. I married three beautiful women but you outshine all of them tonight. And you know why?'

'Because you like my blue dress best?' she teased, knowing blue was his favourite colour.

He laughed, hugging her closer. 'Because you've got it all together, Tessa,' he confided. 'You're not just beautiful. You shine with happiness. And let me tell you it does a father's heart good to see that shining from his daughter.' He dropped a kiss on the curls tumbling over the top of her head. 'Now go on back to your husband. And you can tell him I'm proud of him, too.'

'Because he's made me happy?'

His brows lowered for a thoughtful moment. 'Nick was a good kid. While I thought he was my son he gave me a great deal of pleasure. Whatever has gone on in his life between then and now...I think he's become a good man.' His face cleared into a smile. 'He couldn't have made you happy otherwise.'

A good man...

The phrase lingered in her mind.

It was true of Nick. No doubt about it. But she wondered and worried a little about his two unknown brothers. Were they good men? How would the meeting turn out for Nick? She had argued for it so strongly, but people were always the sum of their lives and the lives of the other two illegitimate sons of Enrique Ramirez could have been very bad.

What did they value?

What did they want?

The party ended. The guests departed. Nick finally did race Tess off to bed where they made love long into the night, idly discussing the party when they felt like talking. Naturally family members eventually featured in the conversation, which led to Tess bringing up her thoughts about their imminent trip to Brazil.

'You know your brothers might be in it just for their inheritance, Nick.'

She was very aware that hopes could end up hurting badly. There might be more rejections in store for the man she loved.

'It could be an end. It could be a beginning,' he mused, rolling her onto her back and leaning over her to trace her lips with a gently teasing finger. 'They can link their life journeys to ours or not, Tess, and part of that choice will be if we want to link to theirs, as well.' There was no concern in his eyes. 'We simply go. And what will be will be. All right?'

She nodded.

They had dealt with so much.

Of course they could deal with whatever else came up.

Together.

His kiss promised her that.

To have and to hold, from this day forth, for better or for worse...